I0545565

UNLOCKING SHADOWS

Keys to Love, Book Four

Kennedy Layne

UNLOCKING SHADOWS

Copyright © 2018 by Kennedy Layne
Print Edition

eBook ISBN: 978-1-943420-45-2
Print ISBN: 978-1-943420-46-9

Cover Designer: Sweet 'N Spicy Designs

ALL RIGHTS RESERVED: The unauthorized reproduction or distribution of this copyrighted work is illegal. Criminal copyright infringement is investigated by the FBI and is punishable by up to 5 years in federal prison and a fine of $250,000.

All characters and events in this book are fictitious. Any resemblance to actual persons living or dead is strictly coincidental.

Dedication

Jeffrey—There are no shadows with you...only light. I love you.

Cole—You've started the next journey in your life, and we are so very proud of you!

Chapter One

Twelve years ago…

H OPE.
How could an individual still have such an impractical yearning after facing such a malicious, unrelenting evil?

Emma Irwin still desperately grasped at the prospect that she'd be with her family soon. She'd tell them all about the things that people took for granted, such as how much she loved them. She'd apologize to her older sister for acting so childish and to her mother for not doing the dishes like she'd promised this morning. The simplest acts of kindness weren't hard to perform, yet she'd never realized how selfish she'd been until just this moment.

Until she'd found herself in a situation that was her father's worst nightmare.

Emma bit back another sob as the old wooden dock underneath her back jostled her from side to side in time with the storm. The gusting winds from the gale had churned up the lake, and the choppy waves were slamming into the weathered planks. Cold rain was descending from the black sky overhead, washing away her tears as if they never existed.

When a crack of thunder overhead was followed a second later by a streak of lightning, it was a harsh reminder that she was still alive.

Emma shifted so that her bound hands didn't dig into the

small of her back quite as badly. She struggled to free herself from the thick white zip tie secured tightly around her wrists, refusing to accept that she would die at the hands of someone she'd once trusted.

How could he do this to her?

The hard, half-inch wide plastic cut into her skin, a cruel reminder that she was at his mercy.

His muttered curses were drowned out by the torrential downpour, which served her well. He wouldn't be able to hear what she was doing behind him.

The wooden deck jarred abruptly, providing her the momentum to roll forward. Her cheek scraped against the wet, rough plank as she leveraged herself to her knees. The cold rain had numbed her skin long ago, but that could easily have been from the terror that had flooded her system when she realized that a man she'd known her entire life was a monster.

"I'll give you a family of your own."

Emma screamed as he suddenly appeared before her.

"Please," Emma choked out, having strained her voice after he'd all but thrown her into the bed of his truck. "Please don't do this. You know me. You know my family. I *have* a family."

"You were unhappy."

"I wasn't," Emma denied emphatically with a shake of her head, swallowing back the sob that rose in her throat. "I wasn't unhappy. I love my family. I do. I always have."

Emma could have continued pleading, but her frantic claims would have fallen on deaf ears. She began crying uncontrollably. He wasn't hearing anything she said, and he'd even turned away to throw what looked like a pile of chains into a boat that wasn't even his.

Her mind registered his horrific intentions, and she instinctively managed to scramble to her feet.

She ran as fast as she could despite of her wrists being bound, ignoring the rain pelting her face and the wind attempting to knock her off the deck and into the lake. She'd just learned to swim this past summer, but she'd done so with the use of her hands. She'd most likely drown immediately without being able to move her arms.

Adrenaline kept her moving forward, though she blinked furiously to clear her vision so that she could make it to land.

There!

Up ahead.

Headlights pulled into one of the cabins that Birdie rented out to fishermen or families on vacation. She instinctively began screaming, but the rumbling thunder overhead drowned out her cries for hope.

That didn't stop her from trying again.

Unfortunately, it was too late.

"No, no, no, no." He'd grabbed ahold of her wet strands of hair, yanking her back against him with such force that it knocked the air right out of her lungs. She couldn't scream, and she couldn't even cry. "I'm taking you home."

Emma didn't need to be told that she would die if he got her into that boat. She fought his constricting grip around her upper body, kicking and twisting in an attempt to free herself at all costs.

It was of no use. He was too strong, and the lights she'd seen were no longer there.

The hope she'd been holding onto had been doused by the rain and swallowed by the darkness of his soul.

"I'm taking you home where you belong, Emma."

Chapter Two

Present day…

A BRIGHT ORANGE leaf fell slowly from a branch overhead, twirling and dancing in the light breeze until it landed softly on the cold ground. Added to the swirl of autumn colors were vibrant reds and subdued yellows that brought back memories of swinging on a large tire that Dad had strung to an upper limb with a single length of thick, heavy hemp rope.

Gwen Kendall and her brothers couldn't wait until the pile was high enough before they would all jump into the mountain of leaves that had taken all day to rake together. It was as if she could still hear the delightful laughter from the past as she fondly remembered the childhood shenanigans being well worth the trouble of raking the leaves all over again.

"I thought I might find you out here."

"Look at you, solving the most difficult puzzles and winning amazing prizes," Gwen said, tossing a smile over her shoulder from her seat in the tire swing that her father never managed to take down. She wasn't surprised to find her older brother walking toward her with two cups of steaming coffee. "No wonder the town made you sheriff. You always could find every one of us when we played hide and seek in the woods."

"It wasn't that hard when none of you could keep quiet for more than ten seconds at a time." Mitch handed off one of the mugs before he lowered himself to the ground at the foot of the tree. He then leaned against the trunk of the large maple, crossing his legs at the ankles. He made himself comfortable, not worrying about getting dirt on his faded denim jeans. "Besides, the sheriff's position is a temporary assignment until the town elects someone they believe is qualified for the office."

"You keep telling yourself that. You're as good as elected already," Gwen murmured innocently before taking a sip of the rich java that had gotten her through some of the toughest deployments during her ten years in the Navy. Those care packages her parents had sent filled to the brim with her favorite ground coffee beans had most likely saved her life. "Hmmm. This hits the spot. I forgot how cool the evenings could be this time of year."

"The sheriff's position is temporary." Leave it to Mitch to address her witty comment, all the while ignoring the second half of the conversation. He was the most solemn Kendall sibling out of the five, but that wasn't surprising given that he was the oldest. He took his position in the family ranks seriously. "I didn't take an early retirement to find myself in a position that requires me to work more than forty hours per week still wearing a uniform and carrying the same weapon. Been there, done that. I even got the t-shirt."

Gwen would have asked how his hip was holding up, but Mitch would only have shot her an irritating glance. He'd most likely unfold his large frame and stalk back into the house if she so much as brought up the subject of the pins holding his pelvis together. Instead, she took another sip of coffee as she used her shoe to gain traction on the worn piece of barren ground underneath the swing so that she could spin and face him.

If he could pick and choose what to focus on in this discussion, then so could she. Her brothers never should have kept such a world-altering secret from her, especially Mitch.

"You could have at least called to give me a heads-up about Mom's final wish so that I wasn't bawling like some newborn baby in front of Dad," Gwen scolded lightly, only to receive a raised eyebrow. She was the only one of her siblings who couldn't achieve such a superior expression. It was irritating as all hell. "Don't give me that look. You know that Dad hates it when I cry."

"I also know that you were well aware of what Dad was up to before you ever drove into Blyth Lake," Mitch said wryly with a shake of his head before taking a drink of his coffee. "You think I don't know about that?"

He was right. She had known that their parents had purchased each of their children separate properties in their hometown. It had been their mother's dying wish to have all of her children back in Blyth Lake, Ohio to raise their own families. Gwen's chest tightened at the thought that Mary Kendall would never get to meet her future grandchildren…nor see any of her children marry.

God, it still hurt to be without their mother. Gwen doubted she'd ever get over losing such a wonderful example of a matriarch to such a horrible disease. Talk about the complete package. She would have been the best grandmother ever.

Gwen cleared her throat before Mitch caught on that she was having a hard time returning to their family homestead without their beautiful and genuine mother at the helm.

"What can I say?" Gwen shrugged with a small smile. "Lance is a horrible liar. Always has been. He's as easy to peel as a grape. One phone call was all I needed to know that something was up with his homecoming, so I made a few discreet calls of my own to find out what was going on."

"And you ruined Dad's surprise for you."

"Did not," Gwen countered, recalling how excited her father

was when he'd spotted her fireball red Jeep Rubicon coming down the lane. "I played it off perfectly, and he was none the wiser."

The last thing Gwen would have wanted was to hurt her dad's feelings. He'd done his best to make today special, and he'd succeeded with flying colors.

Gwen had driven up the gravel lane lined with full-bodied tall pine trees, having rolled the windows down to catch the fresh scent of pine that she'd missed over the years. The sight of their dad—Gus Kendall—standing on the front porch of his two-story yellow house with its full three-hundred and sixty degrees wraparound porch had immediately brought tears to her eyes.

Mom had loved that porch. She used to spend hours out back of the kitchen snapping beans from her garden. Gwen could still feel the sting on her palm from hitting that old screen door on the way out to the back yard, craving the adventure that awaited her on those long summer days.

It didn't take a genius to figure out that Dad was trying to fill Mary Kendall's shoes, of sorts—the most wonderful and loving mother in the world who had always been standing on her beloved porch steps with a dishtowel in her hand, waving it excitingly in the air each time Gwen had visited home.

Gus had a dishtowel in his hand, but he wasn't exactly the *waving* type. Instead, his wide smile that practically bared all his teeth said it all—he was beyond happy that his only daughter was finally home after serving her duty to her country.

Each of her brothers and their newly acquired significant others—with the exception of Mitch, who would most likely remain a bachelor for the rest of his life—had been in attendance for the family barbeque her dad had thrown to welcome her back to town. It had been so chaotic greeting everyone that she'd been fortunate enough to have the commotion keep the tears at bay…until Gus Kendall had handed her the last key, per her mother's wishes.

She didn't doubt that her dad had kept five keys on the same keyring before Noah had arrived in town, being the first of the Kendall clan to drive back over the county line for good.

Gwen was now the proud owner of a small piece of prime ranchland where she would be able to rebuild the old four-stall stable whose bones were more than fit and ready for a new proprietor. She'd be able to own a horse or two and go riding on several acres of wooded trails every day after she got home from putting in a full day at the office. From what she remembered of the property back in the day, there was a half-acre of pasture to turn the horses out in and forested hills of hardwood beyond.

Her father had all but handed over her dream on a silver platter, but there was a vital piece of the puzzle that would forever be missing. Her most experienced riding partner was gone, eaten up by the cancer that had sapped her strength and stolen her future.

"We all miss her, Gwen."

Gwen had to swallow a couple of times before she could speak, which allowed her to promptly admonish her older brother for causing her to be overly emotional.

"Stop it," Gwen managed to say with a forced laugh, blinking away the tears. "I'm serious. We're finally all home, and I refuse to make this a sad occasion."

"That's kind of hard to do with all those numbskulls in attendance," Mitch muttered underneath his breath, his gaze darting to the side. "Those three have been making me very unhappy lately. Do me a favor? Tell them to stay out of what's left of my investigation."

Sure enough, the rest of her brothers converged on Mitch's

attempt to have a little one-on-one time with his only sister. They'd always been close growing up, not that she didn't love each and every one of her brothers individually.

She loved them more than anything in the world.

They were the Kendall clan.

Jace was the middle child, but he wasn't technically the peacekeeper. Actually, there were times she'd definitely call him the instigator. Keeper of the peace was her role, and she took it very seriously. Their mother had once said she would never allow Jace to feel thwarted for being smack dab in the middle of the lineup, so he was either the youngest of three or the oldest of three. It was most likely why he had a split personality—one minute he could be the comic relief and the other he was downright sentimental.

Then came Noah. He was his own person, always doing things he thought was right and to hell with anyone else who thought otherwise. He had a mind of his own. Maybe it was because Noah had always looked up to his brothers and wanted to follow in their footsteps and accomplish something important. Technically, they'd all fulfilled the family legacy of serving their country honorably, but there was always something more to achieve.

Last, but not least, was Lance. He was the baby of the family, although that adjective didn't come close to describing the man who had all but plopped himself down next to Mitch. His infectious smile always kept the mood light, but he also had a dangerous side to him that had made the Marines very lucky to have him when the mission needed a man of action.

But Mitch? He was special. He'd always been her protector, her supporter, and her sounding board amongst everything else that they had going on.

"Dad is sharing Mom's lemonade recipe with Brynn," Lance

said, bumping shoulders with Mitch to get a bit more room against the tree trunk. "She's going to add a twist and some of Pappy Angstroms' lightning to make a new drink to sell at the Cavern. Kendall's Ole Summertime Lemonade."

Gwen allowed Mitch to carry on the conversation, still taking in the fact that she was now home in the warm embrace of family. It wasn't that much of a stretch to learn that Lance had gotten back together with Brynn Mercer. After all, they'd been high school sweethearts and destined to be so for their entire lives.

It was Noah and Jace falling into two rather serious relationships that had her stumped.

"Anything new on the investigation?" Jace asked quietly, causing Gwen to catch Mitch's glare of irritation and bring her around to the conversation at hand. "Shae's parents headed back to Michigan after the service. I'm sure the drive was hell knowing that the person who'd killed their baby girl is still out there hiding somewhere, free to do as he pleases."

Gwen truly wanted to heed Mitch's request to steer the conversation away from a murder case that had basically rocked the town of Blyth Lake, but she couldn't bring herself to force her way in.

She hadn't been here when Noah and his new love—Reese Woodward—had inadvertently discovered a body in the wall of his newly acquired homestead. Apparently, everyone had assumed the decomposed body had at first belonged to Emma Irwin. The teenager had gone missing twelve years prior, but Gwen had already left town to start her life in the Navy by then.

From the updates she'd been receiving from their father, it had clearly come as quite a shock to everyone to find out that the identity of the victim had been a young girl by the name of Sophia Morton from another county altogether. Coincidentally, she had been Reese's cousin who'd been thought to have run away from home over a decade ago, or so most folks had thought.

Gwen couldn't imagine unintentionally finding a long-lost relative dead and hidden inside a wall of a random house. She would want answers, too.

"No, there's nothing new to report," Mitch replied solemnly. He grimaced in distaste when his coffee no longer tasted the same. Neither did hers. "We're still waiting for identification on three of the bodies we recovered from the lake. The remains of Emma Irwin, Sophia Morton, and ten others have been returned to their families. Other than that, law enforcement agencies at the county, state, and federal level are working around the clock to find the son of a bitch responsible for killing all those young girls."

"Don't forget Whitney Bell," Noah added on, having taken a seat in the grass no more than five feet from where Gwen sat on the tire swing. "At least her father can now have some peace knowing that she's buried next to her mother and not lost like all those other girls were for so long."

Fifteen bodies had been found in the lake where they'd all swam in the summer as children. Mitch had referred to the site as a killing ground. It was hard to imagine that laughter and enjoyment had taken place near the surface, all the while underneath their feet had been a gravesite of so many young women who'd gone missing over the years.

"Leave it to all of you to be tangled up in some murder investigation," Gwen said, tossing Mitch an apologetic glance as she joined in on the discussion. She couldn't help it. "I mean, Noah and Reese found Sophia's body after taking a sledgehammer to a wall. Lance discovered pictures of the missing girls in the basement of his new home, and Jace—"

"Hey, don't jinx me," Jace warned as he held up a hand. It was as if he were warding off some evil that she was directing his way. "Nothing happened on my property, and I intend to keep it that way, come hell or high water."

Every one of the Kendall siblings stared at Jace as if he'd grown his hair long. That was how ludicrous his claim sounded, given that the woman who'd returned to town to find out what happened to her sister had been in the direct crosshairs of the killer.

Evidently, Jace and Shae had begun a relationship that had turned serious over the course of the last few months. Maybe love did have blinders.

Gwen didn't begrudge Jace any happiness, or any of them for that matter, but he was way off base if he didn't believe that the Kendall name wasn't permanently linked to this investigation.

"I think Shae's horrific experience was more than enough to qualify you being part of the case there, stud." Gwen hated to point out the obvious, but Shae was lucky to be alive. The two of them had been friends since they were kids, only being a year apart in age. Even though Gwen had been a bit surprised that Jace had fallen for Shae, there was no better woman suited for him. "How is she doing, anyway? She seemed happy at dinner."

"Physically, Shae's fine. She had the stitches in her scalp removed a while ago. Unfortunately, she's still having nightmares a couple of times a week, but we're making it through alright." Jace picked up one of the numerous leaves that had fallen from the maple tree overhead, feigning interest in its pattern. It was clear that he still struggled with almost losing the woman he loved to an evil son of a bitch whom no one had known existed until this past summer. "I want this fucker dead, Mitch."

"And we're doing all we can to bring him in," Mitch reassured his brother, not missing a beat. "Detective Kendrick handed everything over to the feds, for the most part. A fresh set of eyes are now combing through the mountains of evidence. Truthfully, I think we've scared the perp underground for the time being. We've discovered his playground, and he's off sulking somewhere. He's probably not so sure of himself as he has been."

Gwen didn't want to ask what would happen when the sick individual who murdered fifteen young girls decided he was done standing in the corner. She also wasn't going to have her homecoming overshadowed by something she couldn't control. Not for the time being, anyway. She would have added on that she wasn't a part of the investigation, but that wasn't technically true—what happened to one Kendall affected them all.

"Who's volunteering to work on my renovations with me?" Gwen asked, finally giving Mitch the reprieve he wanted. "Dad explained that the old Graber homestead needed a bit of tender loving care to make it habitable. I'm not going to be able to do all of the renovations myself with my new firm opening its doors on Monday. Anyone got any ideas?"

Gwen had done her best to make the transition to Ohio as smooth as possible for her clients. She'd rented the perfect space on Main Street, right next to the bank that had welcomed her presence with open arms. The town of Blyth Lake tried its best to keep the doors of small businesses open, and so far, they'd succeeded beyond most folks' dreams.

She was much more than a financial adviser, having developed an uncanny ability to read the market. She could also do a lot for the younger residents in setting them up for the future, as well as instruct the older townsfolk in safer investments for their retirement.

Unfortunately, there was little time to renovate a home when a thriving business needed all her attention.

"We've got you covered." Noah was the only one who had remained standing, though he was using the thick trunk of the maple tree to lean against. "Chad Schaeffer will be handling most of the renovations, seeing as Miles and I have been cleared to return to the lake to work on those cottages. We're meeting him out at Lance's house tomorrow morning before driving over to your new place to access the most immediate needs. Dad had Chad out to the property a couple of days ago, so he already has an idea of what needs to be done."

"Why Lance's house?"

Gwen was honestly surprised that they were meeting Chad Schaeffer on a Saturday morning in the first place. Didn't contractors like that operate Monday through Friday? Maybe because Noah was now part of the company, they were making an exception of sorts.

Schaeffer's Contracting & Flooring was a family business comprised of a father and three sons. Two of them—Clayton and Wesley—had branched off and tried to take their trade to the city, leaving only Miles Schaeffer behind with his youngest son at one point.

All that went to hell when Clayton believed that the police thought he was the one responsible for the murders. He'd acted impulsively and totally irresponsibly when he attempted to burn down Lance's house to destroy evidence that he'd been the one to do the renovations, thus giving the real killer the opportunity to leave behind damning photographs taken of the victims.

"I want to show you and Chad what Lance has done with his flooring. It will give you an idea of what we could do in your living room." Noah flipped Lance the bird when their younger brother held up his arms in victory. "Shut it. Everyone has to have a good idea once in a lifetime. Even a blind squirrel finds a nut once in a while."

Lance mouthed some not so very flattering words their brother's way.

"What was the outcome of Clayton's case?" Gwen asked, not recalling if she'd heard the final conclusion to that chapter of the story. "I still can't believe that you didn't press charges, Lance. I mean, come on. He tried to burn your house down. You were inside when he tried to set it on fire."

"The man made a stupid, drunken mistake. He acted without thinking." Lance grimaced, but he managed to choke out the words anyway. "I'm trying to take the higher road."

"What he's trying to say is that Brynn is taking the high road for the both of them," Mitch said, his tone telling everyone exactly what he thought of Clayton Schaeffer.

"I heard that," Brynn called out from behind them, though she didn't seem to take offense at Mitch's observation. "Apple pie and my spin on your mom's lemonade are next up on the menu. I've been sent down to collect all of you wayward siblings."

Gwen was older than Brynn by three years, so they hadn't been friends back in high school. That technically meant nothing, though, especially given the size of the town they'd grown up in. Gwen recalled the pint-sized blonde losing her parents when she'd been a teenager and being taken in by Rose and Tiny Phifer. The couple had raised Brynn as their own, giving her the love and stability the lost girl needed to become the fine young woman she was today.

Brynn laughed when Lance tugged her arm, knocking her off balance so that she joined him on the ground.

"Mom's lemonade?"

"Yes," Brynn replied softly, as if understanding how important it was to keep traditions alive. "Although your dad has come up with the perfect name for the new drink I'm going to introduce to the patrons—Mary's Medicinal Ade."

"That's absolutely horrible." Mitch wasn't one to mince words. He stood with his now empty coffee cup, most likely with every intention of coming up with a new designation for such a special drink. "I'll give him a couple of ideas."

"You better let Shae do it," Jace recommended, very proud of the new woman in his life. Shae was currently traveling back and forth to the hospital where she worked in Michigan, slowly transitioning her patients to other psychiatrists in her practice. Her goal was to be working at one of the hospitals in Cleveland before too long. The larger city was a bit of a commute, but living in such a quaint little town made it worth the hassle. "You'll only piss Dad off if you tell him that his idea sucks worse than limeade."

Gwen carefully stepped out of the tire with the help of Noah, who was now holding onto the thick rope so that it didn't sway too much as she gained her footing.

"Is Reese still here?"

"Yes, she was the one cutting the apple pie and making sure I get the biggest slice," Noah replied with a happy smile. "She also talked Dad into giving her Mom's recipe. There's a fundraiser coming up for her classroom at the school. Listen, about Clayton…his court appearance was postponed, but it doesn't look like he's going to serve any jail time."

"Is he going to be working on my house?" Gwen wasn't too sure she was comfortable with such an arrangement. The man had attempted to burn down their baby brother's home, and she didn't much care for the man's lack of character. Lance could have been killed, and she didn't give a damn if that hadn't been Clayton's intention. "I'll be honest with you, Noah. I don't feel comfortable with him working on my place."

"Clayton went back to the city, so he won't have anything to do with your renovations. He and Wes also lost the contract up at the lake. Miles has been in talks for Wes to come back home, but you can imagine how hard that decision is for Wes. He feels like he's abandoning his brother in Cleveland to fend for himself."

"I'm surprised Miles would want to take Wes back into the fold after everything that's happened." Gwen had heard how the Schaeffers were all but torn apart when Clayton and Wes left the family business. Disloyalty to one's family was a mortal sin in these parts. "Honestly, I'm having trouble with the fact that you would want to work with any of them."

"The Schaeffers are good people, Gwen. One bad apple…"

Now this was the Noah she loved—the loyal compatriot and friend.

"You're my brother. I trust you. If that means your new business venture is going to be handling my home renovations, then so be it. I expect top notch work, though."

The only Schaeffer that Gwen knew on a personal level was Wes, because they'd been in the same class. Clayton was older, and Chad was at least two or three years younger than she was. Both had different sets of friends and ran in different circles. She made a mental note to speak with Miles Schaeffer about the company's finances. It would be nice for her brother to have a 401k or some type of savings account where the business kicked in a percentage from their profits.

"Chad is going to be the project manager onsite. I'll be up at the lake now that Rose has transferred the contract for those new cottages to Miles."

Gwen had to smile, because her last memory of Chad Schaeffer was a skinny boy with freckles, dull brown hair that curled at the ends, and braces. She'd heard that he had gained weight and joined the varsity football team in his junior and senior year, but she'd been long gone by then.

The few number of times she'd visited back home had been spent with family. It was astonishing that she'd never run into any of the Schaeffer brothers, though she had seen Miles quite a bit either at the diner or the tavern when she'd been in town.

There were a lot of neighbors and old friends that she'd love to get reacquainted with, and she now had all the time in the world. The pace had definitely slowed when she'd crossed the county line.

Today was about family.

She wrapped an arm around Noah's waist, resting her head against his shoulder as they walked together toward the house. Their mother might not be here in person, but her spirit surrounded them in every bloom of her flowers, every leaf on the trees, and every bird singing their beautiful songs.

"Welcome home, Gwen."

"You, too, Noah. You, too."

Chapter Three

"**W**OULD YOU STOP looking as if you're being forced to walk to your own grave, son?"

Chad Schaeffer ignored his father's attempt at making this upcoming job anything other than what it was—pure hell. It was probably a good thing that he was going to be left to his own devices while his dad and Noah were up at the lake with a crew of eight men to help out on the lakeside jobsite.

Noah promised to be a great addition to the company, but Chad didn't want anything to do with the Kendall family. It wasn't anything personal, but it also didn't take a genius to figure out pretty quick that the family was somehow connected to the evil schemes of a serial killer who had targeted Blyth Lake.

It was best to leave such people to the proper authorities to deal with. It was a cancer he didn't want to touch his family any more than it already had.

Chad's older brother had gone and gotten himself caught up in the horrifying mess, tying the Schaeffers to the Kendalls' mess in the first place. Clayton was not known for making the best choices, but he'd gone way too far this time. He almost cost Lance Kendall his life in his drunken stupidity.

It was a wonder the FBI hadn't come knocking on Chad's door after that fiasco, considering he'd been tied to the original missing person case of Emma Irwin. He'd been one of the last people to see her alive twelve years ago. Now that the feds were in charge of most of the investigation, he expected that his family would get drawn in further.

Memories and guilt rose like the dust he'd stirred up entering this old abandoned house.

Damn it.

This was exactly the reason he didn't want to be involved with the Kendalls any more than necessary—which lately seemed to be every damned day. He'd pack his shit and move if he didn't love his hometown. He didn't remember much about his mother, but he did remember her always saying to his father that things had a way of working themselves out if only he'd have the patience.

Well, Chad had endurance in abundance.

"Listen, I might need to borrow Jake now and then. There are things that will go much easier with another pair of hands." Chad purposefully steered the conversation in another direction. He sure as hell wasn't going to be drawn into a discussion with his dad about Clayton and Wes rejoining the family business after what they'd done. It was better to concentrate on the job at hand, giving time for things to settle. He surveyed the damaged hardwood floor worn from years of abuse, but it wasn't anything he couldn't fix. As a matter of fact, he was looking forward to having a bit of time to himself. "I'm figuring two weeks of honest hard work here, max."

"Chad, you can't keep—"

Thankfully, the ringing of his cell phone stopped Miles from venturing into dangerous territory where he didn't want to tread. Yes, he damn well would keep avoiding the conversation as long as he liked. Technically, he wasn't avoiding anything. He was being patient. Biding his time. Right? In the end, it didn't matter what his thoughts were on the matter. His father had the final say on whether or not Clayton and Wes came back to work for

Schaeffer's Contracting & Flooring.

Chad's preference didn't mean a goddamn thing.

He truly believed neither one of his brothers deserved a damned thing.

A quick look at the display confirmed his guess as to who was calling.

"Noah, I got your message about Gwen running late. Lance let me take a look at the unique trim he'd made for the perimeter of his floor. I can do something similar for her, and I'm already at her place. Dad just dropped off some power tools at the house and is now headed to the diner for breakfast."

Miles shook his head in disappointment, but Chad steeled himself against any recourse. He dealt with his own bag of bricks on a daily basis, and he sure as hell didn't need any more. His dad rubbed the back of his neck before accepting that now wasn't the time to push the issue. He slowly made his way to the front door in defeat.

Noah's voice drew Chad back to the phone conversation.

"I'm sorry about the delay. Gwen received a business call right as she and Dad were leaving the house. We're on our way to her property now."

"Take your time. I have to complete my detailed survey, anyway," Chad said, reassuring Noah that there was no hurry. There were things that needed to be done before he met with Gwen and confirmed some of the things he, Gus, and Noah had talked about last week. "I'm going to go through the place to see if we missed something on our initial list—anything that might require immediate attention. We already have power and the place didn't burn down, so that's a start."

Chad didn't end the conversation too soon, giving his father time to walk to his work truck so there wasn't any chance of being drawn back into a conversation about his brothers. The strain between all of them had only grown worse over the last few months. It would eventually come to a head, but it wasn't going to be right before he started a job and was about to commence demo of the damaged materials.

Chad would wait until he was done with Gwen's renovations before giving his opinion on how the company and the dynamics that came with it could work going forward. If Clayton and Wes were going to rejoin the family business, Chad would need time to accept the choice that his father had made for him.

He truly didn't believe that his father was willing to sacrifice one son over another.

There was a way this could benefit all of them, but only if everyone was willing to put some boundaries into place. The reckless actions of his brother had placed the family business at risk before, and Chad wouldn't stand for his brothers putting themselves first again.

"Hey." Noah's deep voice coming through the line grabbed Chad's attention away from the front door. "I appreciate you doing this. I know there's been quite a bit of tension between our families after what happened with Clayton and all. You could have easily pawned this off on Jake, but you're the one I trust to oversee what Gwen needs to get started on the right foot. After all, she's my only sister. She deserves the best."

If Chad hadn't known any better, he would have sworn there was a listening device implanted in the living room. He resisted the urge to look around. The house wasn't quite as large as Lance's place, but the design was rather similar, considering the era in which they were built. He hadn't seen Gwen in many, many years, but anyone who'd been blessed with such a gift would be thrilled to have such a piece of property.

"It's not a problem, Noah," Chad reassured his new business partner. There was a restructuring in their near future, but it had to remain status quo for the time being. "I'll see you and Gwen in a bit."

Chad disconnected the call and shoved his cell phone back into his pocket before slowly analyzing the room in front of him. The years hadn't been kind to the façade of this place, but her bones were as solid as a rock. It was a decent-sized living room with a staircase to the left if one were entering the front door. The old wooden railings on these longstanding homes never ceased to amaze him for all their intricate detail.

Back in the day, people took pride in their work and always provided as much workmanship as the job could afford.

Unfortunately, all the walls had been slapped with a fresh coat of white paint. He'd have to tear up some of that work to see if he needed to strip the existing drywall to get at the wiring or the plumbing in case it needed to be brought up to code.

That left the floors to be another major project in need of some TLC. This type of heavy oak flooring usually resurfaced just fine, but it took a mountain of work to get it to look the way it should.

Gus had the electricity and gas hooked up to the house a few days ago, but the utility company intentionally hadn't opened up the main gas valve to the house without an inspector giving the okay that everything was as it should be. There hadn't been enough time to completely check everything out prior, and Gus hadn't been given a definitive date on Gwen's return until recently.

From Chad's understanding, she should have been home weeks ago.

The property had a well that needed to be serviced. Water wasn't an issue other than needing to have a series of prefilters installed and a premium soft water system to get rid of the unwanted minerals and that horrific sulfur smell. Most folks nowadays wanted access to a reverse osmosis water system for their cooking and drinking supplies.

Chad would need to get two different subcontractors for the wellhead and the plumbing of the water systems. As far as he knew, he could have all that taken care of this week if the various businesses had openings in their schedules.

Power was the first requirement, and he needed to get an electrician in here to check out the box, along with the services to the rest of the house and the outbuildings.

Chad took a minute to himself as he surveyed the house, picking up the coffee he'd poured into a travel mug before leaving his place. The stillness of the home had a peaceful quality that was an integral part of these old properties. It was one of the reasons he'd never moved away from Blyth Lake. Nothing else had ever settled his soul like restoring these historic, beautiful homesteads that had been an important part of the region's history for the last seven or eight generations.

He wasn't sure how much time he had before Noah pulled in the driveway, so Chad grabbed his tool belt and began lugging some of the heavier tools upstairs. There were three bedrooms and two baths, and all of them needed some amount of work.

One of bedrooms faced toward the east, so the morning rays would make a warm bed even warmer once the sun got over the horizon. Much like downstairs, the one consistent item in the bedrooms that needed attention were the old oak floors.

Gwen would most likely want some type of plush carpet in the bedrooms, while restoring the hardwood in the hallway and down the stairs. He'd prefer to refinish the hardwood floors and drop rugs beside the beds, but that was him.

As for the bathrooms, new counters would be needed if she wanted to update the décor. The tile was a mess. She was coming in from some major city, so he guessed at what her preference was in regard to her living space.

Chad lightly brushed his fingers over the railing as he descended the steps, noting that the wood had been painted white most likely years prior when that was a thing. It was a shame, really. Covering up something so beautiful was a crime, but it could be easily rectified with some time and patience—both of which he had plenty of and was willing to provide at a price.

The distant sound of an engine and the popping of gravel indicated that Noah and Gwen had finally arrived. Chad hadn't gotten to go over the kitchen or the basement, but he'd already spoken to Noah about getting the kitchen, the main bedroom, and the upstairs bathroom done first so that Gwen could move in as soon as possible. All he was waiting on was for her to pick out the carpet that she'd most likely use to cover those beautiful wood floors.

The front door had been left open, so all Chad had to do was open the screened door that had a purpose years ago before the house had a central air conditioning unit installed. Now? It wasn't needed this time of year, but it was nice to have the house breathe in some fresh air after being shut up and abandoned for so long.

He stepped outside, noting that the temperature was still quite cool. The scent of fresh cut grass hung in the air, courtesy of Gus hiring one of the local teens to get the yard presentable before bringing Gwen by to see her new abode. The only eyesore was the stable, which was in desperate need of a total rebuild.

A quick glance at his watch showed it was now going on nine o'clock in the morning. The sun wasn't strong enough to raise the temps out of the fifties, but if they were lucky, the high of the day might hit sixty-two if the rain held off this afternoon.

Chad raised a hand in greeting as two vehicles pulled up

alongside his red Dodge Ram. Noah's F150 pulled in behind, but it was the red Jeep Rubicon that caught his interest. The Wrangler had to belong to Gwen, and he could already tell by her color choice that they were going to be friends.

He was younger than Gwen by a couple of years, so he never really hung out with her group of friends back in the day. He imagined that she'd most likely frequent the tavern, seeing that Brynn was the proud owner after Tiny and Rose had signed the bar over to her earlier this summer. That place had a renewed sense of energy, and Brynn had been hitting it out of the ballpark with all the updates she'd been working on lately. Not to mention the live entertainment by some of the more popular local bands on the weekends.

One glance at the woman who'd stepped out of the Rubicon had Chad changing his perception. Friendship might not be the only thing on the table.

There was no way in hell this amazing woman was the Gwen Kendall he remembered from high school. That girl had been rail-thin, long black hair that hung to her waist, and overly tanned skin that had most likely been acquired by cooking herself outside with baby oil. That had been a trend back then, if he recalled correctly.

But this woman?

Gwen Kendall sure as hell didn't belong in Blyth Lake.

Shiny black hair that resembled the luminous color of a raven was flawlessly cut to frame her sculpted face. Her porcelain skin surpassed the most beautiful porcelain doll, while her full lips were smoothly covered with red lipstick that basically begged to be worn off. She also had a figure that rivaled that of any obsolete hourglass.

Gus and Noah's abrupt manifestation by Gwen's side was a wakeup call, and Chad had to clear his throat so that he could call out a greeting. That last thing he needed to do was act like an imbecile in front of Gwen while Noah and their father looked on.

He was a grown ass adult, but even he agreed the word *ass* should be emphasized considering his reaction.

One would think he'd never seen a beautiful woman before.

Chad discreetly rubbed his eyes as he leaned against the white pillar of the wraparound porch that had been painted to draw in buyers, though that time was well over a few years ago. The previous owners only had so much discretionary income to put into the house, so they had chosen mostly surface elements to polish the curb appeal, as they called it. Which was a great reminder that the external shell didn't always represent what was on the inside. For all he knew, Gwen's time away had stolen her shy demeanor and she was hell on heels—not that she was wearing heels out here today.

"Chad, it's been a long time."

He was so fucked.

Gwen smiled brightly as she looked up at him from the sidewalk, her melodic voice like honey being slowly dripped down his skin. Fortunately, she waited until she'd taken the two steps to be by his side to hold out her arm in greeting. He now had a better rein on his responses and didn't even let on that the faint scent of vanilla enveloped him as her fingers ever so slowly closed around his.

"It's good to see you back, Gwen."

Chad was grateful for an excuse to release her hand, extending his arm to Gus. The older man was friends with Miles and had been for years. It was good that there didn't seem to be any animosity between the two regarding Clay's recent stupidity. Their families were now too connected and entwined for there to be any residual hostility...or so Chad kept telling himself that on a daily basis.

"Are you here by yourself?"

Gwen's question threw him a bit, but he caught himself before showing his surprise. He didn't miss Noah's wince, though. There had apparently been a conversation about Clayton's recent lapse in judgement, and of course, Wes and Chad were guilty just by association. It didn't matter that their older brother made his own choices.

Gwen had clearly made up her mind about the Schaeffer men.

If that's how she wanted to play it, then that was fine by him.

"Yes," Chad replied, letting her know in no uncertain terms by his steel tone that he was capable of keeping this professional moving forward from this point. "I was going to be the one handling your project, for the most part. If you'd prefer someone else heading up the renovations, I'm sure Noah can make a good recommendation."

Gwen Kendall was the prime example of how one shouldn't judge a book by its cover. He should have known better, too.

Well, he got her message across loud and clear.

Chad would do them both a favor and stay far away from wherever she showed her pretty face in town.

Chapter Four

G WEN RECOGNIZED HER mistake almost immediately, but it was too late to take the words back after they'd tumbled from her lips. She had no excuse other than to admit that Chad Schaeffer had taken her by complete surprise.

He was...

Well, he was nothing like the awkward boy she used to see in the halls of their old high school. He was all...well, he was all man.

Gwen might even go as far to say that he was quite possibly the most attractive male specimen she'd ever set eyes on, and that was saying something, considering she'd worked closely with a huge number of servicemen in the Navy for over ten years.

Chad would have been a sophomore when she'd been a senior, but he'd never stood out to her back then.

Now?

It was as if she'd overlooked a diamond amongst the coal in her own backyard.

All he needed was a white Stetson Rancher and a pair of Tecovas work boots to be on a billboard for some upcoming rodeo event. She'd never considered a plaid cotton shirt and Levi blue jeans as being sexy, but she was quickly changing her mind.

HIs brown hair curled in all the right places, while his deep green eyes reminded her of the beautiful, vibrant color of a rainforest she'd once visited during her time in the service.

That wasn't technically true.

Right now, the rich green hue of his eyes had turned the color of a hostile sea threatening to overtake her small launch and crash it on the huge rocks of the seawall surrounding the bay. She'd obviously upset him when that hadn't been her intention. The distressed glances she was getting from her father and brother weren't helping any, either.

"Chad, I didn't mean—"

"I know what you meant, Gwen. It's fine." Chad nodded toward the men before walking toward the screen door. "I'll be inside rounding up the tools that I already brought in."

Chad didn't have to add that he wouldn't be waiting for her decision on whether or not he'd be the one to do the renovations, though none needed to be made.

Damn it.

She absolutely hated when things didn't go her way. Her day had been mapped out with the exact timeframe for each stop that she had on the list she'd made last night. It was rare that she ever varied from the detailed schedules she set for herself.

But those infrequent occurrences did happen every now and then, and she was now left behind to pick up the pieces.

"Gwen, what the hell was that?" Noah demanded, running a hand through his hair in frustration. She commiserated with him, but he took it one step further. "Chad didn't deserve that crap, and you're lucky he isn't already in his truck and out of here. I work with the Schaeffers, for Christ's sake. They're good people who had nothing to do with Clayton's impulsive actions."

She didn't need a lecture from her brother when she already felt like shit.

"One, don't speak to me like you know what I'm thinking,"

Gwen warned her brother, tilting her chin to show that she had nothing to be ashamed of after that confrontation. This slight misunderstanding was easily rectified if Chad would only give her ten seconds to explain why she'd asked the question in the first place. "We're not back in high school, and I'm not your little knock-kneed sister anymore. I'm well aware that Chad, Wes, and their father aren't responsible for Clay's choices. I didn't ask if Chad was alone out here at the house because I was worried about Clayton's whereabouts."

"She's right, son." Gus glanced worriedly toward the front door, obviously upset that Chad had taken her inquiry personally. "When we were driving up the lane, Gwen thought she saw someone near the old corral. She was a bit thrown off a bit when Chad appeared on the porch out of the blue, seeing that his truck was the only vehicle parked in the drive."

"I'm sure it was nothing," Gwen brushed away her father's concern, wishing her current problems were so easily eradicated. She sighed in resignation. Her day had not started out anywhere near as pleasant as she'd expected things to go. She never should have taken that phone call. "It was probably a shifting shadow or something in the wind."

Noah's concerned gaze was drawn to the barn and corral, but he made no move to head in that direction. There was no reason to, considering the serene view in any direction off the wraparound porch. She'd overreacted due to all the stories she'd heard last night about the underwater graveyard less than a mile away from where they stood.

"I'll go inside and—"

"No," Gwen said softly with a shake of her head. She didn't need her brother to take care of her mess. "I need to explain myself to Chad, and you going in there like some high school guidance counselor will make him to think you're covering for me."

This wasn't exactly how she'd pictured her first time seeing her new home. Her parents had basically handed over her dream of her own place on a silver platter, and instead of showing her dad how appreciative she was of such a gift…she'd upset the one man who'd shown up with the right tools to polish her rough gem into a work of art.

"Dad, it's beautiful. Absolutely beautiful. I don't know how to thank you, but I do know that we'll have a rotating schedule of poker games, dinners, and celebrations at everyone's houses so that you can see how much we appreciate all you and Mom have done for each of us."

Gwen meant every word, too. She'd driven slowly down the gravel lane so that she could appreciate the scenic beauty that surrounded them. The somewhat tamed wilderness reminded her so much of the driveway leading to her childhood home, which told her that was one of the very reasons her father had chosen this particular property for her.

She was a sucker for maintaining the sights, sounds, and smells attached to memories from the past. The lane leading up to the house had all of those senses covered as if it were twenty years ago.

Driving through the other end of the pine trees scattered in the midst of full-bodied maples and oaks had dawned her new home that she distantly recalled visiting a time or two when Pamela Graber had invited some of the girls over for a sleepover. Her father would always be out on his tractor mowing the lawn and waving as they pulled past.

To say that the view of the two-story house had taken her breath away was an understatement. There was no doubt that the house needed a bit of work, as well as new siding on the barn and a new roof. That didn't include all the repair the corral needed, but the overall state of the structures was solid enough to be saved.

This was her home—the place where she would hopefully one day raise a family.

"I knew you'd love the property." Gus gestured toward the corral out back, but his fond smile told her that Mary Kendall was on his mind. "Do you remember when your mother would take you and Jace to go horseback riding? You always had to have Maggie Mae. If she wasn't available, you refused to go out for your lesson. Your mother would get so frustrated with your insistence on that one old horse."

"Maggie Mae was special," Gwen said softly, recalling how soft the mare's white mane was after having her hair brushed. She used to pretend she was riding a unicorn through a magical field of faeries, when in actuality they were just colorful, seasonal wildflowers native to the area that she would later come to appreciate. "Very special."

"Well, I thought you could finally have a Maggie Mae of your own."

Gwen's throat constricted, so she stepped into her father's embrace and held on a little longer than necessary. He now felt the need to be both mother and father to all of them, and she realized it couldn't have been easy for him.

It was times like these that needed to be cherished. Unfortunately, her mother wasn't here to reap her share of the reward. Gwen should have come home a lot sooner than now, but it was too late to treasure what time Mary Kendall had left.

She was gone.

Those tentacles of guilt began to wrap around Gwen, threatening to crush her for the selfishness she'd conveyed over the years.

Being the only girl in the family hadn't been as easy as one would imagine. She'd been protected her entire life. First, by a father who adored his daughter. Second, by four brothers who considered it their duty to ensure their sister's safety. There had been times she hadn't been able to breathe in high school, so she'd used the excuse of the family legacy to escape.

It had taken the loss of their mother to make her realize that she'd left behind everything Mary Kendall had stood for—family.

"I love you, Dad."

When Noah muttered something underneath his breath about her being a spoiled princess because she wouldn't ride any other horse but Maggie Mae, she instinctively lifted her knee-high boot and connected the flat heel to his shin.

His *oomph* was all she needed to experience that distinct zing of satisfaction.

Yes, they all should have come home sooner.

"I'm going to walk around the property while you go speak with Chad." Gus removed the toothpick from his mouth after she stepped back. His small frown deepened the lines on his weathered forehead. "I know you believe it was a trick of the light, but I'd rather be sure considering what's been happening recently."

"Noah can join you. He needs to walk that last comment off," Gwen said with feigned innocence, ignoring that her brother had leaned down to massage his shin. He'd deserved it, and she wasn't about to apologize for her behavior, either. She hadn't learned how to survive five brothers without having a bit of thick skin or knowing how to subtly get even without her parents being any the wiser. "I'd rather speak with Chad in private, thank you."

"Understood," Gus stated with a nod, putting his toothpick back in place. He motioned for Noah to head down the porch steps first. "We'll be back in ten, pipsqueak. Noah, I think you should give Mitch a call and have him schedule a deputy to drive through the..."

Gus and Noah walked down the porch steps, carrying on their conversation as if the past didn't threaten to draw her back in time.

Pipsqueak.

Her father hadn't called her that for quite some time, and it was somehow like a warm blanket being wrapped around her shoulders after having been out in the cold for too long.

It was amazing to her that one word could make everything right in the world. Not even the upcoming apology she had to issue to Chad seemed overly daunting. She wasn't sure why she'd waited until her dad and brother were a good fifty feet away, but she then walked over to the far end of the wraparound porch and leaned her elbows against the railing instead of going straight inside.

The slight breeze coming across the open field had a slight chill to it that signaled autumn was arriving soon rather than later. She'd heard that rain was in the forecast, but the clear blue sky above gave hope that the storms would remain south of them for the time being. Memories of sitting with her mother on the porch waiting for incoming thunderstorms filled her head, and she hoped that someday she could do the same with her own daughter, snapping beans and talking about which boys at school weren't totally without some measure of saving grace.

It was all but impossible to stop the visions of a porch swing swaying and a huge glass jug of sweet tea brewing in the warm rays as it sat on the railing awaiting dinner. Later, after supper was over and the dishes were done, lightning bugs would dance in the air and bullfrogs would croak to one another in their own language. The chorus of late summer evening music would initiate laughter from the children trying to mimic the sounds.

At this point, it was too late in the season for the lightning bugs, but that didn't mean Gwen couldn't have a bonfire or two as she cleared the broken timbers of the old corral. Not one of her siblings had made her an aunt, but that could literally be right around the corner at the rate they were going.

Only one thing currently stood in the way of delaying those dreams of anticipated family gatherings in the evenings—Chad Schaeffer. She was responsible for how he'd mistaken her inquiry, and it was time she rectified that particular problem. The last thing she needed was to cause dissent between families on her second day back in their hometown.

With a deep breath, Gwen pushed away from the railing and walked across the wooden planks that were roughly still in good shape. Another coat of paint wouldn't hurt, but she'd put that chore off until the coming spring when the paint would have a week or two to cure properly once it was applied. She had the rest of her life to transform this picturesque house into the home she'd always dreamed of as an adult.

She was surprised that the screen door didn't squeak as she opened it, but the interior was as stifling as she'd thought it would be after having gone empty for such a long time. She'd heard that the Grabers had sold the property to an older couple a few years after she'd joined the Navy, but places like this would always be referred to by the original owner's surname until one put his or her own stamp on it. It had been that way for as long as Gwen could remember.

She stopped in her tracks, the screen door hitting her in the back as it tried to close behind her.

Wow.

She mouthed the word after her eyes finally adjusted to the darker tint of the living room. There was one window overlooking the front porch and two on the right-hand side that gave a clear view of the busted-down wreck of a corral. Well, they would offer an unobstructed view once the dirt was wiped from the windowpanes and the corral was rebuilt.

Numerous lists began to automatically form in her mind of the various things that would need to be done to restore such a magnificent home. Had it really looked like this when she was a young girl?

"Beautiful, isn't it?"

Gwen startled at the sound of Chad's rich voice. She hadn't realized that he'd been sitting on the second step of the staircase, drinking what was probably coffee out of an old Cleveland Brown travel mug that had seen better days. His green eyes appeared black from where she was standing, but she didn't need to be any closer to realize that he was still miffed by her earlier query. She also noticed that most of his tools were now collected at the bottom of the staircase.

"I fell in love with the place when I saw the old dented mailbox." Gwen wasn't so sure Chad would listen to what she had to say if she immediately launched into an apology, so she took a different tactic. "Did you see the two large oak trees on either side of the entrance to the driveway? For some reason, I don't remember them being there when my parents would drop me off here to play with Pam."

"We don't see things as adults the same way we saw them as children."

Gwen didn't think he was talking about the oak trees, but she wasn't quite ready to debate his brother's actions. Instead, she looked down at the floor underneath her boots.

"This floor could be stunning, though I'm not quite sure why the railing was painted white." Gwen tossed a glance of distaste at the peeling paint on such an intricate piece of wood.

Who would do such a thing to a work of art like that? "Are those horse carvings?"

"I'm pretty sure they were, but we won't know for certain until someone takes the time to strip the rest of the paint off." Chad was still watching her rather closely, but she didn't want to invade his personal space. He had an underlying vibe that caused her to be a bit restless. "Unless you'd rather leave it painted."

Gwen didn't like to be pushed, but it was clear that Chad was done with useless chitchat. She tucked her hair behind her ear and nodded, accepting his decision not to drag this out. She'd never meant to offend him, but she wasn't sure an apology could fix it.

"Dad and Noah are taking a walk down by the corral." Gwen crossed the floor so that she could look out the window. The dust wasn't as thick as she'd thought it would be, so it was easy to spot Noah coming out of the barn. He wasn't going to be happy that she hadn't succeeded in smoothing things over. "I thought I saw someone down by what's left of the fence, which was why I asked if you were here alone. You should know that Clayton and that entire issue never crossed my mind."

Gwen waited for Chad to say something, but he remained silent. Agitation set in that he was making this situation more difficult than was necessary.

"You—"

The rest of her words caught in her throat as she was brought up short. She'd turned around to tell him that she'd like for him to continue the renovations, but he'd somehow quietly crossed the floor without her knowing.

"Is that your way of saying you're sorry?"

Gwen couldn't tear her gaze from his. He was studying her like she was stranger, which technically she was. But he'd grown up with her younger siblings, worked with one of her brothers, and therefore knew her by association.

Right?

The layered filth on the window couldn't stop the sun's rays from shining directly on Chad as he stood a mere two feet in front of her. The stifled air somehow became even more claustrophobic as she finally recognized the hidden impression for what it was—sexual attraction.

"Having four brothers taught me to never show weakness to anyone," Gwen responded lightly, tightening her hold on the keys in her hand. The last thing she needed to do was muddy the waters more than they already were. "You should know how that is having two brothers of your own, but I'll clarify for both our sakes. I'm sorry if I caused you to think I didn't want you working on this project. That was not my intention."

There was a flicker of excitement in his green eyes that she wouldn't have seen had he stayed on the steps. Her heartrate accelerated a bit, but common sense won out. Chad was playing with her, but she'd participated in this kind of game before. The stakes weren't hers. They were Noah's, and if giving a little ground meant making her brother happy, then so be it.

The last thing she wanted was to make Noah's new job harder than was warranted all because she'd gotten into a battle of wills with one of his new partners.

"Apology accepted," Chad murmured after a long pause, holding out his hand to seal the act of contrition. Her fingers tingled before her palm ever touched his. "Welcome home, Gwen."

Chapter Five

"I NEVER SHOULD have taken this damn job."

Chad drew the wheat flavored beer through the neck of the bottle, not obtaining the satisfaction that usually flowed once it hit his bloodstream. He chided himself for not doing the smart thing earlier this morning when he'd had the chance. He'd been given the perfect excuse to simply get into his truck and drive away. Instead, he gave Gwen Kendall the opportunity to smooth things over and wrap his ass in a sling.

"You could always back out," Irish suggested before walking toward the dartboard to retrieve his three darts. The hint of a tattoo could be seen at the edge of his rolled-up sleeve. "I don't know the Kendalls very well, but it seems to me that trouble follows each and every one of them folks a little too close for my taste. I'd keep my distance, if I were you."

Irish was relatively new to town.

He'd taken over the local garage after old man Delaney dropped dead of a heart attack earlier this year. It had happened so suddenly that no one had even blinked at the quick sale of the old mom and pop repair shop.

That was until the quiet newcomer had arrived in a beat-up old Chevy muscle car.

Strangers weren't exactly welcome in most small towns if they weren't just passing through. It had taken some time for the residents of Blyth Lake to warm up to Irish, and some still weren't too sure about his unannounced arrival.

Irish hadn't been related to Ed Delaney in any way.

That in itself was a red flag for most folks.

Chad overlooked it, because Irish was just looking for a fresh start. That much was obvious. Who was Chad to deny a good man a blank slate? His need for peace in a small town no doubt came from serving in one or both of the recent wars. Irish had never confirmed that guess, but his overly watchful demeanor made it more than apparent. The way he carried himself was a dead giveaway.

"I had the same sentiment." Chad set his cold beer on the table, not bothering to get up from his stool. He wasn't in the mood to play darts tonight. There was no doubt his aim would be off, and he wasn't allowing Irish to win another round because Chad couldn't get his head on straight. "There's too much discord in this town right now, and the last thing I need to do is to drag my family's name back into the daily grist mill."

There was no sight of that redheaded reporter who liked to hang around and try to pretend she could blend in with the locals. Brynn had all but tossed the reporter out on her ass not too long ago. As far as Chad knew, Charlene Winston had never shown her face at the Cavern since.

It did make him wonder where she'd landed and who she'd been trying to befriend to dredge up the local's viewpoint.

"You're too involved."

"I've lived here my whole damn life," Chad reminded Irish wryly, scanning the faces of those friends and family who'd already staked out their seats for the live entertainment that Brynn had scheduled for Saturday night. "It's kind of hard to separate myself from my own neighbors."

"You just didn't try hard enough. Trust me, it can be done."

"Obviously, I'm not a pro like you."

"I could always teach you." Irish smirked. "It's not that hard."

Irish's number one rule was to keep to himself while conducting business, and he succeeded in that endeavor by a bloody mile…maybe even more. Folks around town had all remarked how Irish was nothing but business at the garage and said as little as possible when discussing how he'd be fixing their vehicles.

"You and I both know what your major issue is, man. Let me be the first one to reassure you that you're nothing like Clayton. You got that? Your old man certainly isn't going to tell you, but someone sure as hell does." Irish set all three of his darts down in the middle of the tall table they'd chosen to occupy near the back. He'd been about to take a seat when the front entrance opened to reveal a stranger in a suit. "Well, shit. If that ain't a fucking fed, I'll eat my hat. I'm going to use the head. Grab me another beer, would you?"

Chad quietly studied the suit who was making his way to the bar. It was still relatively early in the evening, only going on six-thirty. The live band didn't start playing until nine o'clock, so the bar would be packed by eight with everyone looking to grab the best seats. If this agent thought he'd make more headway than Detective Kendrick, he was sorely mistaken—suit or no suit.

It was like watching a train wreck.

Gus Kendall, Jeremy Bell, and Chad's father were all sitting at the end of the bar in their usual seats. Calvin Arlos, the owner of the local hardware store, always sat to the right of them.

Technically, the only man who'd had his name practically etched into the back of his seat was Jeremy Bell. He'd been an alcoholic all his life, but that had all changed this summer when his daughter had been abducted from his house one random evening and killed.

That was a tragedy that would give anyone a wakeup call.

Then there was Jimmy Web, who was technically related to the Kendalls by marriage. He was at least four stools away from the other men, but that's how he preferred it. He and Gus had some bad blood between them due to the dearly departed Mary Kendall, but Chad had only heard third party accounts of why that was.

One thing about this town?

Never believe what was being said, unless everyone agreed. Even then, it was an iffy proposition.

Sure enough, it was Chad's own father who'd sent the agent scurrying around on a wild goose chase. The suit walked over to where Harlan Whitmore and Chester Mayer sat with their wives at a table near the front of the makeshift stage.

Chad shook his head in disappointment, wondering where his father got the notion that alienating the new investigator that the FBI had put on the case would serve any good purpose.

"I've already called Mitch," Brynn muttered, bringing with her two bottles of beer. She set them on the table while collecting the empties. "You should know that the agent is asking for you by name."

"Me?" Chad's day was just getting worse and worse by the minute. What the hell had he done to deserve this bullshit? Oh, yeah. That's right. He'd been the idiot who'd hosted the fucking party out at Yoder's farm that had been the catalyst for some nut job to go on a killing spree that had continued for over a decade. He still couldn't think of that night without imagining Emma Irwin being dragged through the woods to her death. "Thanks, Brynn. I'll take care of it."

He was certain it wasn't good for business to have a federal agent casing a bar on a Saturday night. The locals were already on edge, and having their personal time stained by the evil that had infected their small town wasn't helping any.

Chad pushed back his chair, accepting his fate.

He had no doubt that this was about Clayton's role in Whitney Bell's murder. It was a wonder that Jeremy was even speaking to Miles, given that their kids had been casually involved at the time of her murder. It was one of the facilitators that had Clayton losing his shit and trying to destroy what he thought was some kind of evidence found in Lance Kendall's basement.

"What's going on?" Tiny Phifer asked, reaching out to stop Chad from walking by. He and his wife, Rose, had been the previous owners of the Cavern before selling it to Brynn—their previous ward and now full-time daughter. Tiny was what everyone considered a gentle giant at six feet and six inches tall…until someone messed with those he loved. "Brynn looks concerned."

"Apparently, the federal agent who's taken over the case thought the best course of action was to show up at the tavern on a Saturday night without informing Mitch of his plans." Chad shifted his stance, uncomfortable with what Harlan and Chester might be saying to the outsider. It was bad enough that his own father had sent the FBI Special Agent on a wild goose chase. "It's nothing to worry about, though. I'm the one the agent wants to speak with."

"Maybe you should talk to a lawyer first," Rose interjected worriedly, never one to keep her opinions to herself. Chad wasn't real thrilled that she'd stuck her nose in his family's business to begin with, but he did understand that her heart had been in the right place. "And Chad? I'm sorry if I—"

"It's fine," Chad reassured the older woman with a small smile. What's done was done. He couldn't take back that Rose thought it would be smart to bring his brothers back to town for a job up at the lake adding on to the row of cottages that brought in quite an income for this duo. "Clayton's mess is his own, and it most likely would have occurred whether or not he was working up there for you at the lake. I know you thought you were mending old wounds, but sometimes scars are best kept as reminders of our mistakes."

Chad patted Rose's hand that she'd rested gently on his forearm.

Irish was wrong when he said Chad was too involved with the town.

Honestly, he wouldn't have it any other way.

These people were like extended family to him, and that was important when blood relatives were selfish pricks who didn't give a shit what happened to their own damn family.

"Let me know if you need anything," Tiny frowned, deepening the lines on his dark forehead. He considered himself the town's protector, so the mass grave had sent him reeling. The fact that the killer used part of their property as a means to transport the bodies only added to the man's guilt. "I'm ready for all of this to be done and over with."

Weren't they all?

Ever since word got out that there had been fifteen bodies found at the bottom of the lake, rental business for the Phifers had taken a gigantic nosedive.

The town itself was thriving, of course.

News of a serial killer drew strangers in for some strange reason.

Reporters were practically crawling out of the woodwork, amateur detectives had blossomed out of every crack, and a book writer or two had shown their faces once it had been confirmed that a serial killer had made Blyth Lake his home. One couldn't find a spot at a decent bed and breakfast for fifty miles in any direction.

"Excuse me," Chad said, interrupting whatever Harlan and Chester had devised to keep the federal agent busy so that Chad could make good his escape. "I'm Chad Schaeffer. I heard you were asking around for me."

The agent's lips compressed in a thin line and his jawline became taut. He wasn't too pleased that the locals had given him the runaround. Chad had to suppress his welcome to Hometown, USA. His wit probably wouldn't go over very well, and the last thing the Schaeffers needed was another sibling in the spotlight.

"You're a hard man to track down. I'm Agent Jay Thorne."

"I'd say it's nice to meet you, but I'm sure you can imagine that we're more than ready for this investigation to come to a quick and conclusive end."

"I'm sure you all are."

Chad didn't appreciate Agent Thorne's tone, but it was to be expected given the runaround he'd just undergone in an attempt to conduct a simple interview in an investigation he was trying to close.

"What can I do for you?"

"I'd like to talk to you about Emma Irwin and the night she went missing."

And there it was—his past coming back to bite him in the ass all over again. Clayton involving himself into this mess probably didn't help Chad's cause, either.

Chad had been on the receiving end of Detective Kendrick's numerous questions. Mitch Kendall had quite a few of his own after he'd taken over for Sheriff Percy. Chad had technically been given a gift that Mitch had become the sheriff right at the time all the bodies had been found. Sheriff Percy most likely would have taken what was obvious without an in-depth investigation and called it a day.

Bottom line? Detective Kendrick and Mitch had treated Chad with respect, though Mitch more so just because of their personal connection and history.

There had been no need for lawyers or red tape, especially when Chad was all for bringing a killer to justice. He considered himself a rather intelligent man, and there was no way in hell he was going to be questioned by a federal agent—especially one with a chip on his shoulder—without representation.

"Of course," Chad replied with a tight smile, reaching for his phone. It wasn't in the front pocket of his jeans. Had he left in the truck? A memory of him placing it on the windowsill in the upstairs bedroom window of Gwen's house slammed into him, banging another nail in his coffin. What had made him think this day could end on a good note? "Why don't we meet at the station where Sheriff Kendall can be present?"

Chad figured something was amiss when Harlan, Chester, and their wives all began to look over his shoulder in disbelief. Nothing could have prepared him for Irish materializing by his side.

"I'll make sure Mr. Schaeffer is at the station in approximately fifteen minutes."

What the hell had happened to the man's motto of *never get involved*?

"And you are?" Agent Thorne asked, clearly not liking this new development.

"Nolan McCleary," Irish answered without hesitation, ignoring the stunned looks from the patrons. Chad was having trouble digesting this bit of news, as well. The country music blaring from the jukebox couldn't hold a candle to the deafening sound of silence that followed. "I'm Chad Schaeffer's attorney."

Chapter Six

"**D**AD, I PROMISE that I'll be home before it gets too late," Gwen reassured Gus, who had reverted to the worry-wart father of yesteryear that she remembered so well. "I'm just going through the house one last time before deciding on my delivery date from my movers."

Gwen hadn't been able to use the ubiquitous Traffic Management Office (TMO), an often-maligned service used by the military that her brothers had just left. TMO was a group of people who the military employed to arrange a move of military members' belongings when those servicemen or women were assigned a new base or were leaving the service to return home.

Unlike her brothers, she'd been out of the service for close to four years now. The moving service she'd hired hadn't been able to use a local storage site due to some insurance snafu. It seemed to be much to her brothers' delight during the welcome home barbeque. They hadn't hesitated to tease her for using some second-rate civilian company to handle her move. It wasn't that they truly meant that, so much as it was to give her grief.

Besides, the Benson twins were damn good at what they did—owning and operating their own local moving company. Unfortunately, she hadn't been able to use their services. The national moving and storage company had come in and packed everything but a couple of weeks' worth of clothes, but she'd had to delay the delivery date upon completion of the hardwood floors.

"You can do that tomorrow." Gus didn't mince his words. She could just picture him adjusting the bill to his cap, getting ready to go to battle. "In case you've forgotten, there's a serial killer targeting women in Blyth Lake."

"I need to head into my new office space in the morning," Gwen reminded her father gently, who was already driving home after his quick stop-off at the bar. He usually only had one small draft beer, which almost always sat on the bar untouched. He never did like to drink if he was driving so as to keep their mother from worrying. Old habits die hard. "I'm paying extra to have a certified IT technician specializing in financial networks come out and make sure all of my servers are online, firewalled, and securely connected to my firm's desktop computers and laptops. Plus, I'm conducting two interviews in the afternoon for an assistant. I need to find someone I can trust implicitly and keep the firm's confidences."

The Cavern was where everyone gathered if they weren't eating at Annie's Diner. The bar was the local watering hole, and everyone out for the evening was usually there. Gus had mentioned that some type of commotion had taken place with Chad when a federal agent had made an appearance out of the blue at the tavern.

In Gwen's opinion, the residents would have to be a bit more indulgent if they wanted their lives to go back to normal. She managed to stop herself from asking about Chad. His personal business wasn't hers, and she needed to stay out of the murder investigation…unlike all her brothers. Besides, her dad would take her casual interest the wrong way. The last thing she needed was for him to start asking when she was going to settle down and make him some grandchildren.

Gwen flipped on the kitchen light while holding the cell to

her ear, her gaze being drawn to the basement door. Lance immediately sprang to mind, and her stomach became somewhat nauseous at the thought that something could be hidden down those stairs. It wasn't that much of a stretch. After all, Noah and Lance had both found disturbing discoveries in their homes that impacted the case.

Were the Kendalls somehow involved in this whole mess?

Gwen didn't believe for a second that her family had anything to do with the abductions or subsequent murders, but that didn't mean someone else didn't *want* to involve them.

"I won't be much longer," Gwen promised, a sense of déjà vu washing over her. How many times had she said that same response when she was a teenager? She did her best to ignore the pull of the memories. "See you soon, Dad. Leave the light on."

It would be useless to tell her father goodnight, when she was absolutely positive he'd be sitting at the kitchen table waiting for her to walk through the door. Hopefully, he'd stay out of the coffee or else he'd be up all night.

Once again, she was forced to accept that old habits die hard.

Gwen walked over to where she'd left her purse on the counter, deciding to wait until tomorrow after the interviews to explore the dark possibilities in the basement. Why disrupt such a beautiful day?

She dropped her phone inside the large opening of her oversized bag before turning around and leaning against the stove. There were numerous appliances that needed to be purchased. She'd already made a list of the brands she wanted Chad to stick to for the utilities, such as an on-demand water heater, a quality water softener for her well water, and the HVAC components. He'd mentioned that he could pick out the appropriate models and then run his choices by her for approval. She could get used to having a contractor onsite.

Gwen was really only concerned with the kitchen appliances. She'd begin her online search sometime tomorrow in between meetings. She'd been setting aside money for years in anticipation of buying a house, and now all those savings could be spent in upgrading the interior, buying herself quality utilities, as well as renovating the barn.

She couldn't prevent a smile from blossoming on her lips in excitement at being able to purchase top of the line appliances she'd had an envious eye on for quite some time. It *was* good to be home, and she was trying her best to suppress the guilt of not returning to Blyth Lake sooner when her mother was still alive.

Gwen did her best to focus on the present and not the past.

She'd already gone through the upstairs and turned out all the lights. She'd been astounded by the progress Chad had already made in the main bedroom, especially after she'd decided to keep the hardwood floors. For some reason, a bit of satisfaction had settled in at his stunned reaction to her disdain of wall-to-wall carpeting.

Why would he think that she would cover up such natural beauty?

A large area rug underneath the bed was all that was needed to add to the rustic décor. She didn't want to change a thing, and she would do everything possible to keep the character of this old house alive and well. After all, she was a country girl at heart. She just happened to appreciate the nicer things in life, as well.

She picked up the pen and small pad she'd been using to keep a list, adding on one of those large wooden butcher blocks that used to be kept in kitchens back in the day. It would be the perfect décor to wrap up the heart of the house, especially after the new counters were installed. Her father had already chosen samples of quartz and granite for her to look at, and it was easy to see he'd had the same vision when it came to restoring such a beauty.

Gwen held the pen and pad close to her chest as she slowly walked through the kitchen, still trying to come up with an idea for the backsplash. She'd have to think on it some more, but something so simple wouldn't prevent her from moving into her new home.

As a matter of fact, Chad had all but promised her that he'd be done with the floors in two weeks' time. His assertion had included the living room, so she could technically have her furniture and other belongings delivered inside of fourteen days.

Her father continued to reassure her that having her stay at the house wasn't an imposition in any way. She was relatively sure that living in such a big house was lonely, but never once had he mentioned moving to a smaller house. She wasn't so sure she or any of her brothers could get him to sell the property…not with Mom's memory still alive in every nook and cranny of their old homestead.

Gwen entered the living room and was standing next to one of the windows that faced the barn when the clouds parted, allowing the moon to shine down on the rickety old corral. The sight was so beautiful that she instinctively crossed the worn floor and opened the front door so that she could look at her new property without viewing it through a smudged and murky window still in need of cleaning.

Before stepping onto the porch, Gwen used the artificial overhead light to write down her need of an interior cleaning crew that did windows. It would be useless to bring one in until the majority of the renovations were complete, but maybe a couple days of work clearing away the debris beforehand might not be such a bad idea. She'd have to schedule the main cleaning crew after Chad was done with the floors, but this way she could knock some of the dust off the place and get a head start on clearing the old boards and scrap metal out of the barn.

The cold air took her breath away, but she didn't bother to go back inside for the light jacket she'd brought with her. She'd only be a minute, anyway.

Gwen was rather impressed with the fact that the planks didn't squeak as she crossed the porch to the far side of the house. She had a feeling that her dad had been out here quite a few times with his tool belt before her arrival.

"Oh, Mom. How I wish you were here to see this," Gwen whispered, wrapping her arms around her middle to maintain what heat she could. "Look at that moon and the way her beams light up the property."

Unfortunately, the weather hadn't held out as she'd hoped. The afternoon rainclouds had moved in, providing a steady drizzle throughout the rest of the day until the front had finally moved its way out of the area. A few clouds remained behind, but they were sporadic at best. A crisp fall evening had set in.

The grass glistened as the moon cast a bluish tint to the blades, while the earthy scent of the nearby woods drifted in the light breeze. There was nothing as fresh as country air right after a good rainstorm. She couldn't wait until the spring when she could plant tons of flowers and add to the woodsy fragrance.

"See, Mom? Who's going to pick out my flowers with me?" Gwen looked over the railing, having already decided she'd mimic what her mother had done at the old homestead. "I'll have to take a picture and take it to Ms. Barmore so that she can help me identify what everything is called. I hear that she still oversees the town's landscaping."

It was silly to talk aloud, make-believing that her mother was standing by her side. Gwen had been taught by her time in the service to be practical, but that didn't mean she couldn't be philosophical about life and death here at home.

Was her mother looking down on them?

Was Mary Kendall in a better place or just gone?

Gwen didn't have the answer, but she'd never stop believing that the dearly departed could still hear the voices of their loved ones left behind. She'd yet to work up the nerve to visit the cemetery. Seeing a name engraved on a tombstone made death seem so final, and she was still dealing with the guilt of not choosing to come home sooner than she had.

Gwen shoved aside the track her thoughts had taken as she pushed away from the railing. She'd been about to head back inside when a dark shadow shifted away from the side of the barn.

A spike of adrenaline shot through her bloodstream.

Her gaze immediately jetted to the same spot as it had earlier this morning when she'd thought she'd seen someone near the corral.

Nothing moved.

Not even the slight breeze left over from the earlier storm moved the blades of grass.

Had she been mistaken?

Was her imagination playing tricks on her?

The hairs on the back of her neck began to slowly rise, and the gradual heat that began to form on her skin told her that she was no longer alone.

Someone *was* out there…blending in with the shadows and standing as still as the night.

Gwen's palm itched to hold a weapon, but she'd only just arrived into town yesterday. She hadn't had time to follow the proper protocol to obtain her carry permit for her home state. Her firearm was back at her dad's place, anyway. Becoming a civilian had been an adjustment, but the financial field wasn't much of a breeding ground of criminal activity. She hadn't had to carry a weapon on her side in a number of years.

That didn't mean she would allow someone to trespass on her property.

Who would be stupid enough to do something so foolish in the midst of an ongoing murder investigation? And one that had to do with a serial killer stalking local women?

A damn reporter, that's who.

Gwen almost called out to whomever was there. There wasn't a damn bit of evidence he or she would find that could tie the Kendalls to this case any more than what had already been written in the press. Her brothers had spilled the beans about a redheaded reporter wrangling her way into conversations at the tavern.

What was her name?

Charlene something. Winster? Winter?

It finally clicked. Winston. Charlene Winston.

Well, little Miss Charlene had chosen the wrong Kendall, because Gwen didn't have to abide by the rules that her brothers had been taught about women growing up. She'd knock the little debutante senseless for messing with the Kendalls.

Never taking her gaze off the area of the barn where she was ninety-nine percent certain the reporter was purposefully shrouding herself in the surrounding shadows, Gwen slowly set her pad of paper down on the railing. She then flipped the pen so that it fit into her hand more like an improvised weapon than a writing utensil.

Gwen purposefully relaxed her shoulders and began to walk back across the porch to where she could descend the three wooden steps. She forced herself to stop and pick up a large rock that was lying in the yard. She didn't want to give away that she'd caught sight of the trespasser. She was just casually gearing up.

She tossed the hefty stone up with her left hand, only to catch it and do the action over and over again. She even stopped to glance back at the house as if she were just appreciating the gift she'd been given by her parents.

The piercing snap of a branch changed everything.

No lightweight woman could have caused such a heavy impact.

Gwen wasn't dealing with a woman, and now she wasn't so sure she was dealing with a random reporter in search of a story at her expense. She had no choice but to spin around, letting whoever was standing in the shadows know without a doubt that his or her presence had been detected.

Was it the man responsible for the mass grave the police had found on the bottom of the lake?

"Who's there?" Gwen called out, forcing the tone of her voice to remain steady. She tightened her grip on the pen and dropped the rock so that she could have her other hand free if the situation called for hand-to-hand combat. "You're trespassing on private property."

In all conflicts, one individual always waited out the other to make the first move.

Gwen never took her gaze off the side of the barn, but she was mindful enough to keep enough of the old broken-down fence between her and her opponent. She kept herself on alert for any possible attack from behind, now truly not knowing what type of situation she was dealing with.

Was the individual alone?

"Show yourself," Gwen called out sternly, taking a small step forward.

Something inherent that she'd relied on during her deployments told her to stop moving, so she once again came to a stop. Her eyesight couldn't distinguish anything in the shadows, but he was there…waiting for her to make a mistake.

When she'd first come out of the house, the crickets and bullfrogs had been in competition to see who could chatter the loudest. There had even been an owl who'd made his voice known.

Now?

Even the wildlife seemed to sense the predator in their midst.

"The only choice you have is to—"

The rumble of an engine cut through the silence.

Within seconds, headlights sliced through the darkness and highlighted her position.

Damn it.

It was then that she heard the sound of heavy footsteps running deeper into the shadows to the stretch of woods in back of the property.

Whoever had been watching her was gone.

"Gwen?" Chad called out after having stepped out of his truck. He'd already shut off the engine, leaving a ringing sound behind as her hearing adjusted once again to the heavy silence. "What are you doing out here?"

Gwen bit back the accusation that he'd just allowed what could have been the killer to escape, but it wasn't like she'd had the man cornered just yet. She swung her gaze back to the edge of the woods, but whomever was in the shadows was long gone. It wasn't fair to take her frustration out on Chad.

"I was…" Gwen let her response drift away in the breeze that had chosen to return. What deep-seated fear had been hidden in this town for so long? She had promised herself that she wouldn't get involved, but that choice seemed to have been taken out of her hands. "There was someone on the property. Chad, what are you doing out here at this time of night?"

Gwen hated that she sounded so suspicious, but there was no reason for him to be here now. She had to force her grip to loosen on the pen as she closed the distance between them, purposefully leaving a bit of space.

"I forgot my phone," Chad said distractedly, not bothering to close the door on his truck. His gaze now fixed to where she'd been looking when he'd pulled into her drive. "What do you mean that someone was here? Someone was in the barn?"

"Next to it, standing in the shadows watching the house." Gwen cleared her throat so that her voice remained steady. For some reason, she didn't want Chad to view her as some helpless female in the face of some unnamed danger that she wasn't even sure existed. "I was on the porch when I thought I saw someone out there."

"And you thought it was a wise decision to confront whoever was stalking you?" The headlights on Chad's truck had yet to shut off. He stepped in front of the beams, preventing her from seeing his expression. She didn't need to, though. His concern and shock were evident. "Did you at least call Mitch?"

Gwen startled a bit when the headlights on the truck abruptly died. Her irritation rose, even though she understood it was an overreaction. She was mad at herself for putting herself in this position.

"No, I didn't." Gwen didn't bother to look back over her shoulder, already accepting that whoever had been on the property was long gone, along with any chance of catching him. She began her trek back to the steps of the porch. "And for your information, I thought that maybe one of the reporters had decided to check out another Kendall property. They have no right to come out here and invade my privacy."

Gwen didn't wait to hear if he had any other questions. She quickly made her way onto the porch, where she took the time to retrieve the pad of paper she'd set on the railing. It was hard not to notice that the crickets had begun conversing now that the danger had passed. She wished it were that easy to go back to her evening as if the past five minutes hadn't happened.

"Gwen, stop for just a second." Chad had quietly come up behind her, preventing her from walking back toward the door. The golden hue of the artificial light shining through the living room window highlighted his worried expression. "Please tell me what happened here tonight."

Gwen wasn't ready to relive that brief flash of terror that had flooded her system when she'd realized she wasn't dealing with that woman reporter who'd been hounding her brothers for anything she could find in order to splash it across the front page of tomorrow's paper.

So, Gwen did what she always did when pushed into a corner.

She went on the offensive and found herself immediately regretting the automatic reflex of lashing out.

"What did the federal agent want to speak to you about tonight, Chad? Do you know something that the rest of us don't?"

Chapter Seven

C HAD RAN A hand over his face in exhaustion, having already dealt with enough people who obviously doubted his accounts of recent past events. He sure as hell didn't need to take that crap from Gwen. She really didn't know him, anyway. She hadn't shown herself around Blyth Lake for over a decade, except for the occasional holiday visit—appearing one day and gone a few days later. She didn't get to stand there in front of him like some holier than thou saint and all but accuse him of keeping some kind of important information from her.

"Chad, I'm—" He'd been about to head into the house, retrieve his phone, and drive back to his place in an attempt to put today behind him. Gwen stopped him, though. She wrapped her fingers softly around his wrist, bringing down his arm so that he was forced to turn and look her in the eye. "I'm sorry. I truly am. I'm on edge, and I seem to be taking it out on you for some strange reason. In case you missed it this morning with the various lists that I've been texting you over and over, I—"

It was then that Chad saw the pen and pad of paper in her other hand. Something had him reaching out to take the articles from her, which was when he saw the impression of the writing utensil in the white, bloodless palm of her hand.

She'd been scared. She'd been gripping the pen so hard that she'd left marks and now the adrenaline was leaving her body as she crashed.

"You're getting better at this apology thing," Chad muttered, drawing the smile he'd been hoping to see grace her lips. They were still the same red color as they'd been this morning, and he had to curb the instinct to see if he could rub off the lipstick. He'd already thought this through, and he needed to stay far away from her for more reasons than he could easily name. That didn't mean they couldn't be friendly. Not quite friends, but maybe something akin to neighbors or acquaintances. Hell, he could use a sounding board after the evening he'd had. "Come on. Let me grab my phone, and then we can head over to my place for a drink. I think we could both use three fingers of my old granddad's sipping whiskey."

Gwen didn't argue, which told him either she was in desperate need of that drink or she just didn't want to go home to her father and spill the details of what happened here tonight. Chad would see to it that Mitch was well aware of what occurred this evening. There wasn't anything anyone could do tonight about some asshole trespassing on the property, but at least Mitch could keep an eye on things and put in some security cameras. A peeping tom would be much less likely to hang when there was a chance of being caught on camera.

Chad held the door open for Gwen, handing back the items he'd collected from her. She didn't say a word as she walked toward the kitchen, her gaze being drawn to the two windows. He flipped on the light above the stairs before taking two steps at a time to reach the upper landing. Sure enough, his cell phone was sitting on one of the windowsills of the main bedroom.

There were quite a few messages from his dad, Wes, and a few other townsfolk checking in to make sure he was alright after Agent Thorne had all but demanded he speak with Chad this evening.

Chad would eventually get back to each and every one of

them to signal the all clear. Right now, he needed to let Mitch know that someone had been on Gwen's property. He created a short note, then hit the send button.

Another message came through before he could slide his phone into his pocket.

Irish.

Well, the man would have to wait.

Chad had been one of the few people in this town who'd given the recent stranger the benefit of a doubt.

And what did Chad get for his acceptance?

A fucking lawyer, of all things.

"Ready?" Chad asked, having made sure all the lights were turned off as he came downstairs. He probably should be grateful that he hadn't had to hand over a month's paycheck to a random stranger for being present during questioning that he'd answered numerous times before. As a matter of fact, he could pretty much recite his answers in his sleep. "Did you check the lock on the back door?"

Chad decided to keep his phone at the ready, because Mitch was sure to respond to the message that had been sent. Gwen was the man's sister. There was no way in hell a deputy wouldn't be out patrolling these grounds in the next ten minutes.

"Yes, it's locked. Chad, why would someone be watching my house from the barn?" Gwen had come out of the kitchen with her purse strap slung over her shoulder. It was one of those oversized leather bags he'd seen the women around town carrying lately. It must be the latest fashion trend. "I arrived in town yesterday. I have nothing to do with this case, and didn't that detective rule out a connection through the real estate deals my dad made? Why would someone be on my property watching me?"

She was referring to Detective Kendrick, who had indeed

ruled out such a connection. That didn't mean a mistake hadn't been made. His last few hours had been spent answering questions for Agent Thorne. That special experience had Chad believing that everyone in town had been put back on the suspect list, as far as the FBI was concerned.

Harlan Whitmore was the town's realtor, and he'd been at the tavern when Chad and Irish had left to go over to the station as directed. But had he remained there with his wife or had he taken her home and headed out here because of something he might have left behind when he had the place on the market?

No. Chad couldn't bring himself to believe that someone he'd known his entire life could do something so horrid.

"We've known Harlan our entire lives," Chad reminded Gwen as he glanced toward the two living room windows. The artificial overhead light was similar to that of a spotlight, making them sitting targets. It would be best for them to take this conversation elsewhere. "I don't believe he has what it takes to abduct, kill, and leave fifteen bodies at the bottom of the lake, if you're asking me. Listen, we should head out of here."

Chad walked to the front door from his position at the bottom of the staircase. He was relieved when Gwen followed suit, removing her presence from in front of the far window. She'd mentioned that she thought it could have been a reporter, and he was hoping that she was right in that assumption.

Charlene Winston wasn't the only reporter in town hoping to scope the story of a century. It could have been anyone out there in the dark near the barn. The police weren't the only ones who believed the Kendalls were strategically connected to the murder investigation. Hell, discovering the killer's gravesite had all but drawn the parasites like mosquitoes to a fresh source of blood.

He trusted that Mitch would get to the bottom of it, especially given that the matter involved his only sister fresh off the bus.

"The reason the police even looked at Clayton was because he did renovations in all the houses, right?" Gwen asked, though there was no accusation in her tone. It was just a well-reasoned question. It eased his concern that she lumped him in with his brother, even though she'd all but said so earlier today. "Does Clayton remember anything out of the ordinary back then? Was someone following him around?"

"Wes and I were working on those properties, too. Neither of us recall anyone acting strange or seeing anything to indicate that Harlan or anyone else we hung around with was involved in something so sick and twisted." Chad didn't take the key ring that Gwen offered as they stepped out onto the porch. He used the key that Noah had given him, sliding it into the slot and ensuring that the deadbolt locked securely into place. "We're assuming the person responsible is from here, but I'm still not convinced of that. It might be a regular tourist that comes here every year."

Gwen hesitated from her spot on the porch, not following Chad down the wooden steps.

"Gwen?"

"I feel like I should stay."

Gwen was more like her brothers than she'd care to admit. Noah and Jace had decided to stay at their places earlier than scheduled, due to the situations that each had encountered. It wasn't a surprise that soon afterward they'd had state of the art security alarms installed in their homes.

"What? So you can sleep on the floor without a blanket or pillow?"

"I've slept with less comfort," Gwen reminded him with a flash of that smile he was coming to really like. She gave a light shrug and finally followed in his footsteps. "You're right. The house will be fine, especially given that you've already texted Mitch and his little army of deputies. Am I right?"

"What can I say? I had a responsibility. I actually texted both Mitch *and* Noah," Chad confessed, walking Gwen to the driver's side door of her Jeep. The wildlife in the field was having a party now that the predator was gone, with all sorts of bugs, insects, and rodents raising hell. They were in their element now, telling him that nothing was amiss. "It wouldn't surprise me to find Noah camped out in the living room with a sleeping bag, shotgun, and a lantern come morning."

"And leave Reese's warm bed? Highly doubtful. Have you seen the way those two look at each other during daylight hours?" Gwen tossed her oversized bag over the steering wheel and into the passenger seat. He didn't miss the not-so-casual glance over her shoulder toward the barn. "You offered me a drink. Are you still extending the invitation?"

"After the night I had? You're damn right," Chad muttered, ignoring the look of curiosity she gave him. She wasn't surprised, which told him that she'd heard something about tonight's events. "Follow me. I have an old jar of Grandpa's corn whiskey from a few years back. Unless you like those—"

"If you say foo-foo drinks, I'll be putting a hitch in your step whilst you get on over to your truck," Gwen warned him before gracefully folding her gorgeous figure into the seat. He once again had to remind himself that this needed to stay in the friendship zone. "I'll be on your bumper, Schaeffer."

Chad had to wonder if Gwen had been thinking the same thing he'd been about the underlying chemistry between the two of them. She'd used his last name as if he were one of the sailors she'd served with in her years in the Navy. That was fine by him. He didn't need the complications. There were lines that shouldn't be crossed, and one of those was with a family member of those men he generally considered friends.

It wasn't long before he pulled around her Jeep in the circular drive, leading the way to his place. He thought back to this morning, when he'd tossed a load of laundry into the washing machine. At least the place was relatively picked up. He lived in town, but that was technically on Gwen's way back to her father's house.

His phone vibrated again, signaling an incoming call.

It wasn't Mitch.

"What?" Chad wasn't in the mood for any more games tonight, but he also didn't want to hear his phone going off every five minutes. "I need time to process the fact that you've been lying to me for close to a year. A goddamned lawyer? Are you fucking kidding me?"

"If you had stayed around the station long enough after your new special agent friend had gotten done with you, I would have given you an explanation."

Irish didn't look anything like a lawyer.

In truth, Chad had him marked for being former special forces or some type of undercover narcotics cop who'd had enough of living life on the edge. His long-sleeved work shirts that he wore when working on cars hid the numerous tattoos that were inked on his arms. He was constantly on alert, tended to avoid any contact with the police, and was inclined to listen a lot more than he spoke to anyone.

Those weren't characteristics of a typical lawyer.

Then again, this proved that Chad wasn't cut out for law enforcement himself.

"I don't want an explanation tonight." Chad flipped on his turn signal so that Gwen could see that they were headed back into town. "I'm going home right now, having a drink or two, and putting all this crap out of my mind until tomorrow. You know why? Because you and I both know that Agent Thorne isn't going away anytime soon. He'll have many more questions and a shitload of other interviews with the inhabitants of Blyth Lake."

"No, he sure as hell isn't done. Not by a long shot," Irish muttered, his tone all but saying that the worst was yet to come. "Stop by the garage tomorrow. I really would like to explain why I kept certain things from my past under wraps."

Chad sighed in acceptance, knowing that Irish probably had a damn good reason for keeping to himself certain facts. Lately, everyone seemed to have secret skeletons stashed away in some forgotten closet.

Was he the only normal one in this whole damned town?

"Fine. But it'll have to be later in the day. I'll be at Gwen's house most of the morning and afternoon knocking out the floors."

Chad disconnected the call, coming to a stop at one of the four-way intersections in town. He could barely make out the tavern, but there were a lot of vehicles still parked outside on the main drag. The place was still hopping, and it would most likely stay that way until the two-thirty closing time.

He maneuvered some of the side streets until he pulled into his driveway, not bothering to open the garage. Gwen didn't need to see the collection of projects he had going on that he wasn't even close to finishing up anytime soon.

Chad turned the key counterclockwise in the ignition, shutting off the engine. He glanced in the rearview mirror and saw that Gwen had parked right behind him. The dome light came on as she popped the door, but for some reason she remained inside the Jeep. He got out of his truck to see what was wrong, but he figured it out by the time he was standing outside the driver side window.

She was jotting something else down in that notepad of hers.

"Are you always this organized?" Chad asked after he'd finished opening the door for her. "I swear you texted me three lists during dinner. I can't imagine what's in that notepad of yours."

"Organization is the key to success in business." Gwen might have believed that once, but he could easily read the doubt in her expression as she sat in the driveway. City life was drastically different than the peaceful slow pace that a small town offered. Her next statement all but confirmed that he'd been right in his assumptions. "This transition isn't going to be as easy as I thought it would be."

"Why is that exactly?" Chad led the way to his front door, ignoring the fact that Tobias Essinger was peering out his front window next door. The man had a bad habit of spying on his neighbors when his nose wasn't in those Zane Grey western books he loved so much. "From what I hear, your new office next to the bank is prime realty."

"Give me that whiskey you promised me, and I'll tell you all about it."

Chad didn't miss the way Gwen was surveying the interior of his house. It wasn't much, but it *was* all his. He'd purchased this small two-story home when he'd turned twenty-one, after having attended a construction trade school specializing in residential housing. Everyone was always in a rush to go to college, and the trade jobs were becoming harder and harder to fill. An experienced journeyman carpenter could make fifty an hour or better depending on the location of the job.

It was a shame, really.

Some of those kids would be happier with a career in the trades.

There were good jobs out there to be had, but most people wanted a white-collar job that didn't result in needing a shower at the end of the day to wash away the sweat.

Chad walked through the living room and into the kitchen, wondering what she thought of his simple design. It was relatively humble, but then again, he was a modest man. The décor was pretty much traditional in nature. He wasn't materialistic, but he did like comfort.

"Did you make this?" Gwen asked after he'd come back with two rocks glasses and an old mason jar filled to the brim with clear liquid. She had one of those loose-knit sweaters over what appeared to be a comfortable t-shirt. It was pulled close around her middle, telling him that he might want to turn up the thermostat. He never liked doing so this soon into the season, but the nights had been rather cold early on. She was leaning over a side table that was up against the back wall. "The craftsmanship is exceptional."

"It should be," Chad said with a knowing smile, twisting off the gold metal screw cap on his family's crowning achievement. "Your father made it for me after I'd seen something similar at Chester and Stella's house. You know, I'm not a total lost cause."

Gwen had already taken the liberty of pouring three fingers worth of sipping whiskey into her glass. He raised his own to his lips as he reminded himself of those lines he shouldn't cross. He considered himself a man of considerable inner strength, but it was becoming apparent that she could be a potential chink in his armor.

"I never said you were."

Chapter Eight

G WEN HAD NEVER been the kind of woman who flirted with men in bars, and she'd never crossed that professional line with any of her clients. In all honesty, she was married to her career and didn't have time for fun and games after hours. What little time she had to herself, she spent trying to decompress rather than wasting it on someone else and complicating her life further.

Maybe it was because Chad reminded her of her childhood when she'd been carefree, capricious, and had never given a second thought to the consequences of any given situation.

Chad made her want that time back, yet in retrospect...she had invested it wisely.

"What happened with you and our newly arrived special agent tonight?" Gwen asked, taking another healthy drink of the homemade whiskey he'd given her in an attempt to cover up her slight misstep. He was a distraction she didn't need right now, especially when all of her concentration needed to be centered on setting up her new place of business. "You mentioned that you needed a drink as much as I did."

"The FBI agent who took over for Detective Kendrick decided tonight would be a good night to get to know one of the locals," Chad replied wryly and with a bit of a shrug. The slight twitch of his shoulder told her that the introduction had bothered him more than he wanted to let on. "He strolled into the tavern a couple of hours before the live entertainment was about to start and decided on me."

Gwen winced at the obvious error. She might have been gone for many years, but there were certain things that would never change in a small town.

"Let me guess," Gwen said, turning on the small wedge of her boot so that she could walk over to the brownish black couch that was made of that microfiber she loved so much. She adjusted the throw pillow against her side before offering up her guess as to what had taken place after such an entrance by a virtual stranger. "Jeremy Bell told him in no uncertain terms that he could walk right back through the doors and never come back."

"He might have done that had Agent Thorne not asked for me by name the moment he arrived." Chad's grip on the glass tightened, and his jaw muscle ticked as he continued to share details of his evening. It was beginning to sound as if his had been worse than hers. "Jeremy and my father decided it would be best to say they didn't know my whereabouts, and then sent the agent over to meet Harlan, Chester, and their wives."

Gwen winced again in response, knowing full well how those two men loved to play with strangers when they came into town.

"Did you attempt to slip out the back door?" Gwen's smile faded when she observed his reaction. She hadn't meant to offend him, but the disbelief that crossed his face told her that he took exception to her question. It was a good thing she didn't tell him that she thought the residents should accept the help being offered by the feds. She couldn't imagine his reaction then. She held up her free hand in defense. "I didn't mean anything by that, but it *is* a Saturday night. Agent Thorne might be in charge of the investigation now, but this is still Mitch's town. I never said he shouldn't be present if one of the residents are questioned by outside law enforcement."

"I don't know what kind of man you think I've become, but I don't run and hide from trouble." Chad finally moved from his place near the side table. He took a seat in the matching overstuffed chair, crossing an ankle over one knee. Gwen had to remind herself to breathe at the intensity in his response. Confidence was on her list of attributes she wanted in a partner. He'd been right earlier about her penchant for lists, but one checked item didn't make Chad Schaeffer the *one*. "I offered to meet Agent Thorne over at the station, with Mitch present for the interview. Like you said, this is his territory now."

"What did Agent Thorne want to know that Detective Kendrick hasn't already produced?"

"Thorne wanted to hear my account of the night Emma Irwin went missing fresh from my lips." Chad took a long draw of his own whiskey, his gaze clouding with what appeared to be remorse. "You see, I was the one who had a keg brought out to the old Yoder place for the party that night. I was the one who threw that last bonfire, which ended up getting her killed."

Chad wasn't telling Gwen something she didn't already know. Her mother and brothers had kept her apprised of the horrifying days that had followed Emma's disappearance. Search parties had been formed, canines had been brought in, and yet it was as if Emma had disappeared into thin air, never to return alive.

Bad things like that didn't happen in small towns like theirs.

Gwen's outlook on that had changed quickly after serving in the Navy.

Evil was everywhere.

"I'm sorry," Gwen replied in her softest tone possible. She would have reached out for his hand in comfort had he been closer. Guilt had a way of devouring a person's soul. She should know. "I'm sure that is a time of your life that you'd rather forget."

"No, it's not." Chad drained half the contents of his glass. "Truthfully, it was a wakeup call not to end up like my brothers, always in their cups. I stopped partying, concentrated on my grades, and then went to a solid trade school that would allow me to contribute to the family business."

"Chad, it wasn't your fault that Emma went missing. She put herself at risk when she decided to walk home that late at night. Evil caught up with her." Gwen was sure he'd heard the same sentiment over and over again, but she felt compelled to say it once more. "If you hadn't hosted that last bonfire at the farm, someone else surely would have. It was the go-to party place back in the day, and the property had been sold to new buyers. It was a sendoff, of sorts."

"Every single teenager in attendance was questioned, but all anyone could remember was that Emma had taken the shortcut through the woods to get back to town. She'd been late for her curfew." Chad rested the mason jar on his thigh, staring at it like the green-tinged glass had all the answers. "The last glimpse I had of her was when she glanced over her shoulder to wave goodbye to Billy Stanton. He'd strung her along that night, hoping to get lucky."

"He was always an asshole. From what I hear, he hasn't changed much."

"He's dating Julie Brigham now." Chad lifted his upper lip in distaste. It was evident he thought Julie was smarter than that. "Such a waste."

Julie had been best friends with Emma Irwin and Brynn Mercer back in the day. Brynn had said something at dinner last night about how Billy was just using Julie as cover, and that it wouldn't be a major surprise if it came to light that Billy had something to do with all of these murders.

It was hard for Gwen to imagine a teenager having the knowledge and forethought to not leave a trace of evidence behind in an abduction and subsequent murder. Then again, it was even harder for her to accept that someone like Harlan Whitmore, Chester Mayer, or Calvin Arlos could carry out such horrid acts of violence.

"My brothers mentioned that Calvin Arlos was a prime suspect for a time." Gwen couldn't imagine the hardware store owner being anything other than kind. He used to hand out candy to the kids who went into the shop with one of their parents. "I also heard that he suffered a heart attack after being questioned by Detective Kendrick."

"Calvin's recovered nicely, but he's lucky he didn't have another setback when it was discovered the killer used his boat to try and transport Shae out to the middle of the lake." Chad lifted his glass in salute. "Nothing like returning home to this whole fucking mess."

A mass of chills descended over her flesh at remembering the sight of the shadow moving next to the barn. It hadn't surprised her to receive a call from Mitch while following behind Chad's truck on the way to his place. She'd all but been reamed out by her older brother for not calling him the moment she'd noticed something was wrong.

"Like I said, I don't really have anything to do with the investigation. My brothers? Well, they have a hard time not getting involved with crap like this." Gwen caught sight of a family photograph that only included Chad, his brothers, and his father. She gestured toward the frame with her glass. "We have that in common."

"Clayton couldn't successfully steal a piece of candy from a grocery store if he tried," Chad professed with a shake of his head. "Wes was always the sneaky one, but neither of my brothers could ever take a life of one of their neighbors. Neither could I, just in case you were wondering."

"I wouldn't be sitting in your living room if I thought otherwise."

"And here I thought you were a risk taker. One of those daredevils. I should have known better after being sent all those lists today." Chad's wink caused a surge of excitement where there shouldn't have been. She had best be wrapping up this impromptu engagement. "It's your turn, Kendall. Tell me why you think your organizational skills are no longer needed for our mutual project."

Maybe the high alcohol content had reached her bloodstream, allowing her to relax against the cushions of the couch. It could have been the fact that Chad had opened up to her first, thus letting the floodgates ajar. Did she feel obligated to return the favor? No, not in the least. That alone told her that a part of her trusted him to keep her confidence.

"It's not so much the organizational skills that I blame for the choices I made in my life. It's just that I purposefully fit my decisions into a little box that my mind created to be independent of my family."

Gwen took a healthy nip from her drink, wishing she could have a little more. She wouldn't, though. She still needed to drive home this evening. And at thirty-two years old, she still had her father sitting in the living room and waiting up for her on a Saturday night. That checkmark she'd made was fading fast, yet she didn't experience the suffocation she'd fought against all her life.

"I'll admit that you lost me."

Chad held up his empty glass as if he'd given a point to her in some fictional game they were playing.

"It's the Kendall family legacy that we all serve our country," Gwen explained, though she wasn't telling him anything he didn't already know.

She took one of her nails and started picking at the uneven bevel in the glass. Once she said the words aloud, she couldn't take them back.

Is that what she wanted?

"Our mind has a tendency to cause situations to seem worse than they really are," Chad said somewhat quietly, as if he understood her plight. "It's similar to what we touched on this morning. We don't see things as adults the same way we saw them as children."

Gwen allowed his words to settle over her. For some reason, they soothed her remorse in a way she couldn't explain.

"I fulfilled the legacy, but I also used it to my advantage," Gwen reluctantly admitted, cringing a bit at the harsh reality. "It sounds petty now, but growing up in a house full of brothers wasn't always easy. My parents did their best to shelter me, my brothers took over that duty whenever I left the threshold of our house, and this small town that I truly love had a way of suffocating me back in the day."

Chad's green eyes lightened a bit as recognition dawned on the direction she was taking this conversation. He nodded his understanding, yet he hadn't been the one to leave all this behind in his rearview mirror.

"Once again, we don't see things as adults the same way we saw them as children." Chad had poured himself a bit more whiskey and drained it immediately. Gwen was only halfway through drinking the potent brew. "You know that families are usually scattered all over the world. Phone calls, video calls, and texts keep us connected. It's not like you cut off all communication with your family."

"I should have been here for her, Chad."

There. Gwen finally confessed to what was in her heart. She would have thought she'd be having this conversation with Mitch, but she'd never been able to get the words around the lump in her throat.

"And you're different from your brothers…how?" Chad wasn't being accusatory. The tilt of his head told her he really wanted to hear her response. "Didn't you just get done saying that you didn't appreciate being treated differently when you were younger? Why should you get to be different now?"

"That's just nonsense psychology," Gwen said with a laugh, admiring that he wasn't allowing her to wallow in self-pity. Her laugh faded quickly. "All of my brothers were still in the service. They had an obligation. I've been out for years, checking off those boxes I'd mentioned earlier when I could have been here."

Gwen didn't have to add on that she could have been here spending more precious time with her mother. When the cancer diagnosis came down, they'd all heard the word…but accepting that fate had been harder to accomplish.

"Creating those mental boxes, as well as those written ones, made you who you are today. That's not a bad thing, Gwen. We live and we learn. It's the cycle of life. We all come to our end in our own way."

"It's foolish to say I thought we'd have more time in that eventuality. I should have come home." Gwen shrugged, deciding it was time to bring this conversation to an end. She was just grateful that she'd made it this far without breaking down into a blubbering mess. "Believe it or not, my father warned me that he'd be waiting up for my arrival tonight."

Chad rubbed the side of his jaw, almost as if he were debating whether or not to let her off the hook after she'd all but bared her soul. He then said something totally unexpected.

"I, for one, like those lists you texted me today. I'm thinking one of those old-fashioned chalkboards can be added to the small wall in the kitchen that's basically wasted space." Chad nodded toward her phone with a smile. "Text that to me, so I don't forget."

"I like you, Schaeffer."

Gwen doubted that she'd ever truly forgive herself for wasting such precious time, but opening up to someone somehow lessened her burden. She'd even started creating an inventory of what she'd need to host those weekly poker nights her brothers had mentioned at dinner yesterday. It was time to make more memories that her mother could view from above.

"Really? You like me?" Chad slapped a hand on his chest and over his heart. "And here I thought—"

Police sirens cut off whatever he was about to say, causing both of them to jump to their feet and turn toward the sound. Chad hit the front door first and twisted the knob before swinging the heavy oak wood open just in time to see the sheriff's vehicle coming to an abrupt skidding stop.

"This can't be good," Chad muttered, stepping out onto the small front porch. "If your brother is here for me, will you do me a favor? Call Irish. He took over Delaney's garage when the old man had a heart attack."

"You want me to call your mechanic?"

There was absolutely no way that Gwen could keep the skepticism out of her voice.

"Turns out, Irish was a lawyer in one of his past lives."

Mitch stepped out of his vehicle, a fierce protective expression on his face that she hadn't seen since she'd come home one day from elementary school and told him that one of the boys had pushed her on the playground. It was a look that the red and blue lights of the siren couldn't camouflage.

This wasn't about Chad at all.

Mitch had discovered something when he'd gone out to her property after receiving that text message from Chad earlier this evening. This wasn't how Gwen had pictured her homecoming, and she'd give anything to go back in time to…well, she would have made a lot of different decisions had she been granted that gift.

"Mitch?" Gwen stepped forward, wrapping her arms around her middle in a move that had nothing to do with the cold. "What did you find out at my place?"

Chapter Nine

C HAD WALKED INTO the diner, not surprised that the place was nearly standing room only at seven-thirty in the morning. There were only a couple of tables to spare and one stool left at the counter. That wasn't totally unexpected seeing that it was Sunday before church. This was one meal most folks in these parts enjoyed eating out on a regular basis.

Of course, the usual suspects had taken their regular spots, though Harlan and Chester were with their wives this morning. They'd taken one of the booths instead of their seats at the counter where they usually ate lunch together during the week.

"Chad."

He turned to catch sight of his father's hand in the air, signaling that he'd grabbed them a table near the back.

Son of a bitch.

He should have known this morning wasn't going to go as planned when it had taken him fifteen minutes to find the keys to his truck.

Wes was sitting in one of the four chairs, looking forlornly into his coffee cup as if his outward behavior would ever have Chad feeling sorry for him. He had about the same chance as a snowball in hell.

"Morning."

"Good morning, Chad."

"Mornin'."

"Coffee?" Molly asked over the chorus of greetings, not stopping as she walked briskly around the counter. Nothing could wipe the smile from her face, though. "And did you hear about Jack? He got that promotion on the construction crew."

"I didn't hear that, but let Jack know that I said congratulations." Clay had hung around with Jack during high school, even though he'd been a bit older. The man had been held back in school at a young age, but no one ever questioned it. Things like that happened in small towns when kids rebelled against learning their lessons early on. "And yes, I'd love some coffee."

"The usual? Your dad and brother already placed their orders." Molly slipped one of the order slips into a metal clip and slapped her hand on the high counter. "Order up!"

"Sounds good."

Chad wouldn't have minded if their conversation had continued a little longer. He'd been looking forward to breakfast before heading out to Gwen's house, but Wes' unexpected presence had soured his mood.

"I heard there was some excitement out at Gwen Kendall's new ranch last night," Miles said, not even waiting for Chad to take a seat. He was still pulling the red and silver chair out from under the table as the inevitable question was being uttered. "Everything alright with the jobsite?"

"Someone painted some graffiti on the side of the old barn. Gwen was going to pull the old siding off anyway. It's a damn shame. It's a waste of weathered barn planking, but most of those old boards were rotten anyway." Chad wasn't about to share details of last night with his dad while Wes was still in attendance. Anything said would get right back to Clayton, and the last thing anyone needed was for their older brother to come back to town and involve himself back into the investigation. "It's no big deal. Like I said, Gwen is having the barn redone with metal siding and a new roof."

Chad hadn't lied, but he sure as hell hadn't told the entire story.

Welcome home had been spray painted on the side of the barn in blood red paint.

Gwen and Mitch had spent a good half an hour arguing over the ramifications of such a violation. Mitch signed Gwen's concealed carry permit application last night and had given her a Beretta M9A3, just like the one she'd used during her service with one major difference—the one Mitch gave her had an extended threaded barrel which accommodated a suppressor.

Against Mitch's wishes, Gwen had all but decided that she was moving into the place on Wednesday, which was the first day the moving delivery service could arrive in Blyth Lake with her household goods. Mitch thought that she should continue staying at their dad's place until they caught the individual responsible—both of them assuming that it was the serial killer.

Chad had to play referee, which hadn't gone over so well with the new sheriff. In the end, Mitch had followed Gwen home. Most likely, the two continued to argue well into the night. Chad had no idea how that had turned out.

"I ran into Deputy Byron outside the diner, and he mentioned that Mitch believes it was that damned serial killer." Wes leaned back when Molly returned with Chad's coffee. She refilled the other two cups, but she was immediately called away by one of the other tables. Had it been slower, Chad had no doubt she would have stayed and joined in on the conversation. "Byron said something about the killer finally coming out of hiding to claim another victim."

"I try not to involve myself into things that are none of my family's business." Chad's dig hit home, causing Wes to shake his head in irritation. "What are you doing here, Wes?"

"Dad invited me to breakfast." Wes shared a concerned glance with Miles, who shifted uncomfortably in his seat. "I'll tell you what I told him. We made a mistake. We want to come back home and be part of the business again."

Chad managed to buy enough time before answering by taking a cautious drink of his coffee. He wasn't sure what Molly did, but the rich brew was hot enough to burn a man's tongue right out of his mouth.

"Chad, don't you think it's been long enough?"

No, he didn't. Not even close. Clayton and Wes hadn't been here during the hard times, when the jobs had all but come up dry due to various reasons that were beyond their control. Living in a small town limited their family business to the county line for the most part, and when times were tough…well, they suffered right along with the people they grew up living next to.

It was one of the reasons Miles and Chad had brought in Noah Kendall. He was an expert in the commercial and residential electrician field, which had kept Schaeffer's Contracting & Flooring from taking more than a few jobs that would have brought in quite a bit of money had they not had to subcontract to someone else.

Surviving meant adapting to the new environment. It was a paradigm shift that would allow them to adapt to a new business model.

"Dad, the final decision is yours." Chad hadn't planned to bring up the idea he'd been working out in his head, but his brother's visit had sped up the timetable. "I've been thinking that maybe you can handle the larger contracting jobs that come in, while I concentrate on flooring, tile, and the like. Let's face it, restoring old floors is what I know best. I haven't wanted to say anything, because I didn't want all the stress to fall on your shoulders. Noah being brought in helped, but having Wes and

Clayton back to share the contracting duties isn't a bad idea."

"Clayton and I have lost quite a bit of business due to the ongoing court case, but we still have a few jobs that need to be finished up." Wes regarded Chad carefully to see if he was serious about letting bygones be bygones. Chad hadn't gone so far as to say all was forgiven, but the talk he'd had last night with Gwen about time lost made him realize that he'd been doing the same thing. "I'm hoping we can wrap things up by the beginning of the year."

The thing about being brothers was that years and years could pass, and siblings would still be able to read each other until the day they died. That kind of understanding never faded.

"I don't think Clayton's ever coming back home, though." Wes now had Chad's full attention, and that of the surrounding tables. His brother didn't seem to notice as he was studying their father intently and waiting for a response. "I'm sorry, Dad. I know you thought both of us would return home, but he's too caught up in worrying about what people think of him and what he did. Clay says he's going to take a job with a construction crew in the city once he's cleared of this mess with the district attorney."

Chad locked eyes with Jimmy Webb.

"You just let him know that our door is always open," Miles said, clearing his throat in a way that told his boys it hurt to hear that his oldest wasn't returning home anytime soon. The way the conversation had been steered, the impact of Chad's proposition didn't sting as much as Clayton's decision. "What is new with Clay's case? Lance and Brynn didn't press charges. I'm sure that will help in some way when it comes to sentencing."

Miles and Wes continued to talk about the pinch Clayton had gotten himself into, but Chad really didn't want to start his day off with such a depressing discussion.

"I'm going to use the restroom before Molly brings out our breakfast."

Chad used his work boots to scoot his chair back, giving him just enough room to stand while not bumping into...damn it. If it wasn't Charlene Winston. No doubt, she'd heard every word uttered. She'd most likely spin Clayton's aversion to returning home to her advantage.

It was a damn good thing Chad hadn't said too much about Gwen and the trouble she'd run into last night.

"Chad." He'd been so wrapped up in going over every word he'd said that he hadn't seen Jimmy try to catch his attention. "Do you have a minute?"

"Sure." Chad didn't take a seat, though. He remained standing, crossing his arms and leaning a hip against the opposite booth that sat empty. Jimmy Webb didn't have that many friends around town. "What's up?"

"How is she?"

Chad weighed whether or not to answer the question that was no doubt about Gwen. Jimmy's fallout with the Kendalls was well-known, but he wasn't a bad man. He was just someone who'd made a lot of mistakes.

Hadn't they all?

"Gwen is fine," Chad chose to reply, believing that she would ultimately reach out to her uncle on her own. "I saw her red Jeep parked on the street in front of her new office on the way over. I'm sure she wouldn't mind a visit from her uncle."

Jimmy nodded his head as if he were taking that suggestion under advisement.

"Is she staying with Gus?"

"For the time being, I guess," Chad responded with a bit of caution. Another look around the diner revealed there were a handful of strangers, most likely reporters waiting for anything that would make a story. "Have you been out that way since the boys arrived in town?"

"No, not yet. Gus and I…well, there are still some unresolved issues between us and how the family handled things after my father's passing." Jimmy apparently had heard enough to satisfy his curiosity about his niece. "How's the project coming along up at the lake?"

"Coming along nicely." Chad glanced over his shoulder to see Molly heading toward their table with three plates loaded up on her tray. "Not a lot of traffic since the police dragged the lake. The cooler weather has moved in, as well. We shouldn't have any problem getting those cottages done before the first snowfall."

"I won't keep you," Jimmy said, also having noticed Molly serving Miles and Wes. "I appreciate you taking the time to talk to me."

Chad hesitated, believing that Jimmy had wanted to say something more. When the man went back to reading his newspaper, Chad had no choice but to make quick work of the restroom. He was back at the table before his pancakes could get cold.

The way his morning had started out, he should have known that was only a precursor of what was to come.

The bell above the door chimed, but it was the following silence that told him not to bother reaching for his silverware.

"Who is that?" Wes asked in a low voice, one of the only patrons in the diner that didn't recognize the suit that walked through the front door with purpose. "And why is he looking our way?"

"Jimmy Webb? I'm Agent Jay Thorne." Chad pushed his plate away, having lost his appetite way before the federal agent made his entrance. "I was hoping you'd have time to answer some questions for me this morning."

Chapter Ten

"**B**ETH ANN, I don't understand why you would want to leave Harlan."

Gwen considered the fallout of hiring Beth Ann Mason. As much of an asset as she'd be, the consequences were almost too high. This wasn't a random city where great resumes were a dime a dozen. The scene around here didn't allow for hard feelings.

Blyth Lake?

Any small pebble thrown in the wrong direction could create a tidal wave instead of a small ripple. Gwen would undoubtedly be accused of luring Beth Ann away from Harlan. Was it her imagination or could she hear the tsunami siren wailing already?

"I need something new," Beth Ann said with a bit of desperation in her tone. It wasn't quite the despair of needing more money, but more the misery that came along with doing the same thing day after day. "Gwen, our families have known each other a very long time. You know that I love Harlan, but I'll pull out every strand of red hair from my head if I have to smell his egg sandwich one more time that his wife packs in his lunch when he doesn't eat at the diner."

Gwen couldn't help but laugh at the mental picture of Beth Ann sitting at her desk and holding her nose in response to the rancid odor of a fried egg sandwich drenched in mayonnaise.

"Plus…" Beth Ann's smile she'd given in return slowly faded, finally confirming to Gwen that something more was the reason for this interview. "Things haven't been the same there since Noah and Reese found Sophia Morton's body stuffed in a wall in their house."

Gwen was already running on caffeine alone. She wasn't sure she was ready for where this conversation was heading. For the first time since she'd branched out on her own and opened her own business, she wanted to be anywhere else. Her new home had been vandalized, and Mitch seemed rather confident it wasn't some teenager on a bender having a bit of fun at her expense.

She didn't truly believe that scenario, either.

The dull throbbing that had been relatively consistent in Gwen's temples became a bit more noticeable.

"Ma'am?"

Gwen welcomed the interruption by the technician she'd paid an additional fee to come out on a Sunday so that she could be up and running by tomorrow morning. She gave Beth Ann what she hoped was an apologetic expression before standing from the temporary grey metal desk built by the bureau of federal prisons that had been left behind by the last tenant. It was the standard fare for government offices everywhere around the country.

"Beth Ann, I won't be but a minute," Gwen assured her, rolling back in the matching chair and gratefully stretching her legs as she joined the technician in the main area for a discussion.

Some of the technician's questions she was able to answer, but a few were going to have to be addressed by the software companies she used for one of her trading platforms. He hadn't been a fan from the start of using shielded Cat 5e Ethernet cabling everywhere. It required some minor additional work to install, but it reduced interference and was more secure from signal interception.

Gwen used the brief interruption to gather her thoughts on what she was going to do about the position she needed filled sooner rather than later. Beth Ann was the logical choice in terms of experience, though the ramifications for her in the local community could be staggering.

And why did Beth Ann have to bring up Harlan's odd behavior? That wasn't very professional of her. Gwen needed someone who she could count on to keep business matters to herself. The personal finances of her customers were private...period. A breach of that confidentiality would undoubtedly close the doors on her firm.

A quick glance around the empty offices gave Gwen a sense of purpose. The server had been set up in a ventilated closet on a standard nineteen-inch rack assembly. The different blades of the system all had a series of blinking lights indicating processor status or connectivity with the various systems.

Not only were the server blades installed on the rack, but the modem and router were rack-mounted, as well. All in all, it was pretty impressive-looking.

The main room off the entrance provided for a small open waiting area with an oak railing separating it from the receptionist's desk. Of course, Gwen had ordered specific office furniture that would complement the oak wood. Along the other wall was a small kitchen area in its own alcove created by the server closet and the back wall.

There were two empty offices beyond that area, with Gwen having taken the larger of the two. She didn't need to bring anyone else on at the moment, but that could change should she see a need for someone with their insurance licenses.

"Do you want the software programs loaded on this station?" David asked, pointing toward the desk her assistant would take out front. "I'm already done in both offices. I also left some zip ties on the windowsill for when your office furniture comes in and you need to route the cords through the desks. We call it dressing the cables, but it's really something you can do yourself when the furniture arrives. Unfortunately, we would have to charge extra for another service call."

"That computer doesn't need the trading platform, but would you please make sure the phone system's software is loaded onto the desktop? And please label the server blade that was set aside for voiceover IP and phone system management." Gwen gave him a bit more instructions on what needed to be accomplished today before handing him the list she'd made earlier of miscellaneous programs she'd like installed on the server for easy access. "I appreciate all this detailed work, David."

"No problem," the technician replied with an infectious smile. He was in his early twenties and had more knowledge about computers than most of the IT guys she'd worked with back in the city. "I'm going to take lunch soon. Is there anything I can bring back for you?"

"Want a job as my personal assistant?" Gwen joked around as she set her hands on her hips.

"Oh, I could never live in a town this small," David replied, causing her to reevaluate her opinion. "I stopped to get coffee at the diner, and the waitress there grilled me like I'd committed those murders up at the lake."

Gwen realized that David hadn't meant to cause any offense with his offhand remark, but that didn't mean he should be so dismissive of those who lived in the area and had lost young girls so dear to them. She chalked it up to his young age and inexperience. She decided to let it go without comment.

"Is there anything else?"

Gwen decided she'd rather be dealing with Beth Ann than get into a discussion where she felt the need to defend Blyth Lake.

"Nope, I'm good for now."

Gwen headed back toward her office, wishing she'd been able to schedule the office furniture delivery for today. No amount of compensation she offered could get the store to change their mind about not hiring a driver and an additional mover for the weekend schedule.

"Sorry about the delay," Gwen apologized to Beth Ann, who was glancing at the display on her cell phone. "Beth Ann, I'm still not sure it's such a good idea for you to leave Harlan."

"I know the other woman you interviewed this morning. I also know that I have more experience than her, hands down." Beth Ann had straightened her shoulders, ready to fight for the position. Gwen couldn't help but admire her go-for-it attitude. "I'm looking for another job regardless if you hire me or not, if that makes any difference to you."

It did, but only in terms of Harlan's resentment being directed at someone else. Gwen wasn't so sure she wanted to be on the receiving end of his wrath. It wouldn't be his alone. In small towns, almost everyone took sides on nearly every issue. She didn't want her homecoming to end up on the receiving end of some feud that she had the ability to stop before it ever began.

"Does Harlan know you're looking elsewhere?" The slight hesitation in Beth Ann's response told Gwen the answer to her question. She tried a different tactic. "Have you thought of who would replace you? I understand that it isn't your responsibility, but we're talking about Harlan. You do owe him some loyalty. I don't believe that you would leave him in such a difficult position."

"Mindy Lipton. She quit her job up at the lake after everything that happened," Beth Ann said, leaning forward and lowering her voice as if she didn't want the technician to hear their conversation. Gwen hadn't closed the door, but it was doubtful that David could have overheard them anyway. "She's younger and probably wouldn't mind the smell of those sandwiches since she worked as a hostess."

"Have you spoken to her?" Gwen could see this working out for both her and Harlan should Mindy want a job inside the town limits. "Is she interested?"

Gwen didn't know Mindy Lipton, but the last name did ring a bell.

"Yes, I have talked to her about it." Beth Ann held up her phone. "I told her I'd let her know how this interview went before giving her a call later tonight."

Gwen sat back in the old grey chair that had been left behind with the government desk, ignoring the squeak that occurred every time she shifted on the grey vinyl cushion. Beth Ann had taken the initiative to see to it that Harlan wasn't left in a lurch. That meant that she had a sense of pride, as well as a streak of loyalty to the man who'd given her a paycheck for the last ten years.

"How about we do this…" Gwen began to suggest, truly wanting this mission to find an assistant who was eager to learn the ins and outs of the financial world to come to an end. The reality was that there wasn't a lot of resumes to choose from. "You go and speak with Harlan, explain that you're looking to grow your career, and then give me a call after the conversation to let me know if you're still interested in working for me."

"You're worried I'll change my mind after speaking with Harlan."

"I am," Gwen replied gently, not wanting to set her hopes

up that she'd filled the position. "Beth Ann, you've worked with Harlan for so long. Do you really want to leave just because of an egg sandwich?"

"You really don't know what it's been like here, do you?"

Beth Ann was no longer worried about the interview. After all, Gwen had all but assured her the position would be hers should she still want it after talking with Harlan. No, this was about something bigger.

"Beth Ann, you—"

"Did you know that Harlan was brought in for questioning because he was the realtor for every single property involved in the murder investigation?" Beth Ann shook her head in a rather hopeless manner. "It wasn't only Harlan, but Calvin and Chester, too. It shouldn't have been a big deal, right? But Harlan and Chester were holed up in the office for hours the day after Clayton Schaeffer was arrested out at your brother's farm. And then the warrant came from Detective Kendrick to see the firm's file on every sale of property over the last fifteen years. Harlan was beside himself. Do you know what it's like to go to work every day for a man who's on edge like that? I love him like a second father, Gwen, but I just can't take watching him stress out anymore."

Gwen pressed her fingers into her right temple, wishing she could stop the residual pounding that not even acetaminophen could eradicate.

"Did you tell this to Mitch?"

"Tell him what?" Beth Ann's brows lowered in frustration. "That Harlan was bursting at the seams that the police suspected him of murder?"

When Beth Ann put it like that...

Gwen would have pushed the issue that Harlan was still technically acting out of character, but she once again had to remind herself not to get involved in the investigation. The graffiti on the barn made that objective harder to achieve, but Gwen had pointed out to Mitch that it was a stretch to believe that a serial killer would come out of hiding to spray paint a message on the side of a barn. It could have been anyone caught up in the high drama of the investigation.

"You're right," Gwen replied, dropping her hand and deciding that she'd let Mitch know about Harlan's behavior. That didn't require involvement if she let it slip during Sunday dinner. "And let me guess. You'd feel disloyal to disclose that information."

"I already feel disloyal for meeting with you, but I need to do this for my own wellbeing." Beth Ann glanced over her shoulder to the open space that would be her domain should she still want the job after discussing the change with Harlan. Her green eyes were alit with excitement when she finally settled her gaze back on Gwen. "You said there was room for advancement, and that you'd cover the exams should I decide to take any of them."

"That's right," Gwen agreed, allowing a smile to form on her lips at the enthusiasm for which Beth Ann displayed about working in the financial industry. "But let's cross that hurdle when we come to it. First, speak with Harlan and make sure this is what you really want."

Beth Ann grabbed her purse and stood, not bothering to offer her hand. Instead, she came around the desk and hugged Gwen tight.

"Thank you," Beth Ann whispered, holding onto Gwen longer than necessary. She patted the redhead on the back in return. "I'll call you tomorrow, after I talk with Harlan."

"Make sure he has his coffee first," Gwen suggested with a light laugh, feeling slightly more confident that Beth Ann would follow through. And with this done right, it could work out for everyone without Harlan holding any grudges. "If I remember correctly, didn't Harlan and Chester always to go into the diner before work for—"

The jingle of a bell reverberated through the office. This space had been used for some type of government farm subsidies with the Department of Agriculture before Gwen had acquired it, and she'd yet to have the bell removed. All eyes were drawn to the man who'd entered her new storefront—a federal agent.

"Oh, this can't be good," Beth Ann whispered, pulling her purse tighter against her side. "That's the agent who came into The Cavern last night."

"I'll take care of it," Gwen replied with a tight smile, gesturing for Beth Ann to step out of the back office. "Please keep me updated on the results of your meeting."

Beth Ann took her lead, which boded well for their future working relationship.

"Of course. And thank you for meeting with me. I'll be in touch very soon."

Beth Ann gave David a wave before nodding a greeting toward the agent. Gwen doubted that David would now leave for lunch on his own volition, considering the noteworthy confrontation that was about to ensue. As a matter of fact, the technician wasn't even pretending to be interested in his job loading software.

"Agent Thorne." Gwen took a step forward, pleased that the man blinked in surprise a couple of times before shaking her hand. *Good.* She wanted the advantage. "It's a pleasure to meet you."

"Detective Kendrick warned me about small towns." Agent Thorne reached into his suit jacket after releasing her hand and pulled out a business card. Was that a small notepad inside the interior pocket of his jacket? She respected such organizational skills. "I just had an interesting conversation with your uncle— Jimmy Webb."

Gwen could play this meeting multiple ways, but the smart- est decision would be to have this discussion in a public area. Technically, she should have a lawyer present. Had the circum- stances been different and she'd been involved in this investigation in any way, she wouldn't have hesitated to shut this interview down.

"I haven't had lunch yet. Have you?" Gwen didn't wait for Agent Thorne to answer. She went back to her office and collected her purse, taking a moment to text Mitch. No matter that the feds had jurisdiction over this investigation because it had crossed state lines in regard to the victims, this was still Mitch's town. She slid her cell phone into the side pocket of the oversized bag that contained her day planner before walking back out of her office. There were still quite a few items on her to-do list, but she could check off lunch while talking to Agent Thorne. "I'm ready."

"Let me guess," Agent Thorne said with a not-so-humorous smile. He had the appearance of every other federal agent she'd met while in the service. With that said, he was here to do a job—to capture a serial killer who'd unknowingly terrorized young girls for over a decade. That alone deserved respect. "You would like to go to Annie's Diner."

"I might have just gotten back to Blyth Lake, Agent Thorne, but there are some things that never change here." Gwen rummaged through her bag until she found her sunglasses. She slid them up the bridge of her nose before continuing. "If you'd rather we do this in private, I would insist that we do it at the sheriff's office with my brother present. But if you want answers, you need to go to the one place where there are no secrets…and that's the diner."

Chapter Eleven

C HAD WIPED HIS forehead with the plaid shirt he'd taken off an hour after arriving at Gwen's place this morning. He'd been working since breakfast without a break, grateful that he wasn't just sitting at home watching sports on the tube.

All he'd be doing in his mind was going over and over what he'd heard Jimmy Webb say to Agent Thorne at the diner—he stood by his account that he saw Emma Irwin running down Seventh Street the night she'd gone missing.

"Damn it," Chad muttered, tossing his shirt to the floor before reaching for the jug of ice water he'd brought with him.

It hadn't been enough that he'd lived with his role in Emma's disappearance for over a decade. He now had to relive the remorse practically every day. Gwen had mentioned last night that if he hadn't thrown that party, someone else certainly would have.

Bottom line?

It hadn't worked out that way, and he would forever see Emma's smiling face as she headed off into the woods toward Seventh. The only saving grace was the fact that her body had been recovered, and she'd been given a proper burial after all these years.

Emma Irwin and the rest of the young girls who had lost their lives far too soon could now rest in peace. The murderer's killing ground had been discovered with all the bodies recovered for identification and internment.

Chad had been about to strap on the kneepads he used when working on floors right as the sound of a vehicle breaking through the trees came from the window he'd opened earlier for some fresh morning air. The temperature was in the high fifties, but the sun shining through the windowpanes had heated the room up by a substantial amount.

He recognized Gwen's V6 engine on the Jeep, but there was another barely distinguishable muffled four-cylinder engine on her tail.

Chad stepped to the window, his already sour mood turning more so with the sight of Agent Thorne parking his pea soup green government owned vehicle (GOV) behind Gwen. He was half-surprised the GOV made it up the drive. They tended to buy the worst performing American sedan they could find. Many of the G10 sedans didn't even have basic amenities other than an AM/FM radio.

What the hell did Agent Fife want now?

Chad certainly hoped the bumbling idiot kept his bullet in his pocket for the foreseeable future.

He toyed with the idea of continuing to work as if he hadn't heard the vehicles, but he relented and reluctantly made his way downstairs. It wasn't that that he was opposed to Agent Thorne doing his job, but he sure as hell could have gone about it a better way than confronting every resident he'd wanted to question in front of the entire town. It was as if he purposefully wanted every local on edge.

Agent Thorne had certainly achieved his goal, considering that his approach to the investigation had the townsfolk once again showing their displeasure. The man had all but branded himself a pariah among the very people he was trying to help, which meant that no one was being very forthcoming with information.

"Gwen," Chad greeted warmly, leaning against the pillar of the porch. He made no move to join them in the driveway. He shifted his gaze to the other individual attempting to illustrate his indifference, letting the man know in no uncertain terms that he wasn't happy with this unannounced visit. "Agent Thorne. I didn't expect to see you again so soon."

"Good morning," Gwen responded with a smile. It was good to see that she'd recovered from last night's events unscathed, but why did she have Junior G-man in tow? "Agent Thorne is back in town today to speak with those left on his interview list. He heard what happened yesterday from Mitch and asked to see the barn."

Chad nodded, removing the handkerchief that he kept in his back pocket. He slowly wiped his hands on the dark rag. Agent Thorne had given Gwen a smile that wasn't quite as professional as it should have been. The small gesture shouldn't have bothered Chad in the least, but the fact was…it left him with the same impression as a new driver grinding the gears in a manual transmission.

"Mr. Schaeffer, I didn't realize you were working on Gwen's new property."

Chad didn't miss how the agent addressed Gwen by her first name, blatantly showing how familiar he was becoming with her.

It was also hard to ignore the implications of his statement.

"Noah Kendall is one of my business partners." Chad wasn't telling Thorne anything he didn't already know. "I'd think it would be rather odd if our company wasn't in charge of Gwen's renovations. Wouldn't you, Special Agent?"

"Agent Thorne, why don't we head down to the barn?"

Chad ignored the curious glance Gwen shot his way, fully believing his hardened tone was warranted. Plus, he shouldn't have to explain himself to her. He stayed where he was and observed the two of them walk down the small path toward the corral and what was left of the barn's siding.

What was it about Gwen that got under his skin?

She was once again wearing knee-high boots, though today they were brown leather. She had on a pair of beige pants that conformed to the curve of her ass in a way that he was hard-pressed not to admire. The cream-colored blouse she was wearing flared out at the wrists, and the soft-looking material rippled with each step she took into the wind.

There was no denying that her physical presence had an impact on him, but it was something more than just a physical attraction.

Her laughter at something Thorne said was caught by the light breeze, spreading the melodic sound like seeds of a dandelion caught in a gust of wind that came across the meadow.

"Fuck me," Chad muttered, shoving the handkerchief into his back pocket. "Get your head out of your ass, Schaeffer. You have a job to do."

He'd been about to head back inside, telling himself it was better to mind his own business, when the rumbling hum of another engine broke through the tree line.

What now?

Within seconds, the tan-colored sheriff's vehicle that was a staple of life in Blyth Lake came into view.

Mitch Kendall.

It didn't take long for Gwen's oldest brother to park the Crown Vic behind Gwen's Jeep. He was out of the vehicle seconds after he'd shifted the car into park, not wasting time as he clipped the keys to his utility belt.

"They've already headed down to the barn, Mitch."

"Join me," Mitch said, the directive not coming across as a request in the least. The man was almost built like a linebacker closing in on an opponent, having a larger frame than the rest of his brothers. His size didn't prevent him from moving quietly over the gravel, though. "I have a few questions."

Chad came very close to ignoring the request and walking back inside, having already made it known to Mitch last night that he didn't want to be involved in the investigation any more than the Schaeffers already had been in the past few months. Unfortunately, doing so would only delay whatever Mitch had in mind to accomplish.

"Gwen was only at my house for a drink," Chad explained cautiously, getting this over with now so that he didn't have to be subjected to Thorne's digs. "Your sister needed to get away from here. She looked like she could use a drink after her run-in with whoever was on her property. It was nothing more than a neighborly gesture."

Mitch remained silent, continuing to follow the path Gwen and Thorne had taken. The duo was still within sight, not having rounded the fence that would take them to the other side of the barn. Chad weighed the pros and cons about falling into step, but he'd already made the decision not to put this grilling off any longer than necessary.

"You're assuming I have some kind of problem with you and Gwen spending time together." Mitch's gaze never varied from the duo ahead of them. "I don't. Not in the least. What I have a problem with is the possibility that this goddamned serial killer has set his sights on my baby sister."

Chad had been in the diner this morning, so he'd heard quite a bit of chatter on and off about Gwen's property being targeted by vandalism. Not once did any of the patrons assume it was anything other than teenagers playing around with another one of their own.

Gwen certainly wasn't a newcomer to the area.

"And what makes you think it wasn't the Keller boys or some other local juvenile delinquent?"

"Do you believe it was Matt and Mike?"

No, Chad didn't believe for a second the Keller boys had anything to do with the vandalism to Gwen's dilapidated old barn. It was the main reason why he'd taken a good thirty minutes this morning to scour the property line, looking for tracks or anything out of place.

He'd found nothing but bent grass.

Whomever it was had stayed off the soft ground where there was a chance he could leave a footprint.

"Gwen wasn't even here when Emma went missing," Chad pointed out, wanting Mitch to clarify why he believed Gwen could be a target.

"No, she wasn't." Mitch slowed his pace, his body language telling Chad that the newly appointed sheriff didn't want his sister or the federal agent to overhear what he had to say. "Look, I get that Agent Thorne is just doing his job. He sure as hell isn't taking my advice on how to approach the residents of this town, but that's his own problem. The feds haven't cut me out completely, so I'll take advantage of the situation as much as I can."

"Meaning?"

"I made a discreet call to an old friend of mine. She went over Thorne's head and asked to be assigned as lead profiler, but there seems to be some politics involved that prevented her from joining the investigation." Mitch shrugged, as if he hadn't just put the woman's career on the line. "I sent her the evidence I had anyway. She owes me one."

Chad wasn't going to pretend to know how politics worked

in the federal government. Truthfully, he didn't care one way or another.

"And this has to do with me...how?"

"You're going to be out here for at least the next two weeks." They'd reached the corner of the wooden fence, but Mitch finally came to a stop. "I'm asking you to do me a favor—keep your eyes open for anything unusual. I don't care if a leaf looks like it's been disturbed and you can't figure out why. You let me know. I'm having a deputy patrol the area hourly, but you're going to physically be here eight to ten hours a day."

"Not a problem." Chad didn't bother to confess that he'd already done so and planned to continue to watch this property carefully while working on the house. For a brief moment, he'd been afraid that Mitch was going to ask that he keep an eye on Gwen. Last night had been nice...real nice. A bit too nice. It wasn't wise for him to continue down that road. "I'll reach out if I notice anything unusual. I'm going to head back to the house. I'll let you talk with—"

"Mr. Schaeffer," Agent Thorne called out, having noticed he and Gwen were being followed. Chad didn't doubt the agent had known all along. "Gwen mentioned that you pulled up in the driveway last night after she thought someone was trespassing on her property."

Again, the agent's insinuation rubbed Chad the wrong way. This conversation wasn't going to end with them being on good terms. For a brief moment, he contemplated giving Irish a call. Unfortunately, that would most likely be construed as premeditation for assaulting a federal agent.

"Yes, Chad was here last night," Gwen responded for him, basically shoving his ass into the fire. What the hell did she think she was doing? It was then that he noticed her smile not quite meeting those baby blues of hers, though. It was good to know that she rated him a bit above Thorne, who was virtually a stranger to everyone else in town. "I'm grateful that he pulled into the driveway when he did. Who knows what would have happened had he not shown up."

Gwen had just displayed a claw or two, causing Chad to let go of some of the tension that had settled in between his shoulder blades. He didn't doubt for a minute that she would have been able to handle anything thrown her way, but she'd shined a bit of light on him that the agent didn't seem to appreciate.

That was good enough for Chad.

"Agent Thorne, may I have a word with you in private?" Mitch didn't appear to like these verbal exchanges any more than Chad. "Gwen and Chad, we'll meet you up at the house shortly."

Chad waited for Gwen to reach him before he turned to walk back in the direction of the house. He had work to do, and it sure as hell wasn't getting done by him standing around chatting with the client and basically being a punching bag for a federal agent.

"Agent Thorne really isn't that bad," Gwen said once they were out of earshot. She glanced over her shoulder. "He's just not a very good people person."

Chad thought about making some joke that the only reason she liked Thorne was for his habit of always taking notes. It had been hard to miss the notepad and pen in his hand as he was shoving them back in his inner suit pocket. But Chad's freedom was no laughing matter, and he sure as hell wasn't going to be railroaded by an outsider looking to score a win quickly before moving down the road.

"He'd throw my ass in jail for littering, if he could," Chad muttered, determined to get back to his work.

The sun was beginning to disappear behind the gathering

clouds, but it would be a while before the rain moved into the area. The unsettled air around them didn't help Chad's mood. His morning hadn't gone as planned, and now here he was being delayed by the one thing that had plagued him most of his life.

"Chad." The rest of the walk to the house had been made in silence, so the light touch of her hand on his arm was unexpected. The contact of their skin had him wishing he was still wearing his long-sleeved shirt. "Agent Thorne and I ate an early lunch at the diner earlier. I heard that you had breakfast with your dad and brother."

Well, it looked as if Molly had shared quite a bit of information with Gwen…and the fed.

"No wonder Thorne thinks I had something to do with the vandalism on your property." Chad hated that the Schaeffers had been given a bad rap over Clayton's bad choices. "Wes has decided to come back to town at the beginning of the year. That was about the size of what happened. Tell your new friend that he has nothing to worry about from us. Clayton has decided to stay in the city."

"Chad, that wasn't why—"

"What do you want from me, Gwen?" They had reached the porch, but it was best that he get back to work. He was beginning to think that finishing this job early would be for the best. He'd keep his word to Mitch, but then it was back to a bit of normalcy. If Chad wasn't careful, he'd end up in Clayton's shoes with a case hanging over his head. "Agent Thorne clearly believes that the Schaeffer family is involved with these murders somehow. The best thing for me to do is keep my head down."

Chad hadn't been expecting Gwen to follow him up the steps, nor did he anticipate the way she'd cut in front of him so that he couldn't open the screened door. The sweet fragrance of her perfume merged with the autumn air for an intoxicating scent.

"I just wanted to make sure you were okay," Gwen said softly, her blue eyes searching his for the answer.

Did she have to be so damned beautiful?

He was still struggling to keep himself in check.

The rest of the tension left his body. Even though it wasn't in their best interests, he'd give anything for them to be able to go back to last night when she'd been sitting on his couch and sharing details of her life. He wouldn't lie. It had been nice to have someone to talk to who didn't judge him for his family's actions.

"I could definitely use another shot of whiskey."

"Eight o'clock sound good?" Gwen asked, not blinking an eye at the subtle invitation. Damn if that didn't make her even more tempting. "Dad's having Sunday dinner at his place, but I'm free after the dishes are done. I'm up in rotation."

Chad was saved from responding when Mitch and Agent Thorne's voices carried in the light breeze, signaling that this somewhat casual visit was about to end.

"This can't be good," Gwen said underneath her breath, stepping away from the front door and closing the small distance to the top step of the porch. "Mitch? What's wrong?"

"We got identification back on one of the three remaining victims we pulled from the lake." Mitch didn't break stride as he continued to walk to his car, telling both Chad and Gwen that there was something more to the discovery of the young girl. He should have known that this day wasn't destined to end well, especially when Agent Thorne's attention was aimed in his direction. "Nora McCleary—Irish's baby sister."

Chapter Twelve

"**D**O YOU EVER sleep?"

Gwen startled at the deep voice that came out of the dark behind her.

"Damn it, Lance." She spun around and would have shoved her baby brother had he been closer. A quick glance at one of the upstairs windows told her that their father was still awake. "You should know better than to sneak up on someone. The last time you almost lost an eye."

"I have a spare," Lance said with a shrug and an infectious smile. Usually, she returned one in kind. Not tonight. "Let me guess. You were spending time with Chad Schaeffer."

"We're just friends. Nothing more." Gwen closed the door to her Jeep as quietly as possible. "What are you doing here on a Friday night, anyway? Shouldn't you be helping Brynn at The Cavern?"

Almost two weeks had passed since Gwen had returned to town, and nothing out of the ordinary had happened besides the barn incident. Unfortunately, it had taken this long to schedule the moving company to finally deliver all of her belongings to the house.

Tomorrow was the official moving day, but there had been a lot of debate on whether or not she should leave the family homestead in light of that one event. It wouldn't surprise her if Lance wasn't here to give her a list of pros and cons—heavier on the cons—to dissuade her decision.

"You have to ruin everything, don't you?" Lance shoved both of his hands in the front pocket of his sweatshirt before he rocked back on the heels of his work boots. "Your housewarming present needed a few finishing touches. Since you're being stubborn about leaving Dad's place, I figured I better have it ready to be delivered tomorrow."

Gwen had already seen the beautifully crafted dining room table her dad and Lance had been working on long before she'd returned to town. It had been hard not to notice the large tarp being draped over a piece of furniture every time she'd get anywhere near their woodshop.

She might have wanted to see what kind of wood they'd used in order to choose the butcher block for the kitchen. She might have looked under said tarp, but no one had been the wiser.

Unfortunately, she'd taught all of her tricks in finding their Christmas presents to her brothers when they were younger. Lance was well aware that she was impatient when it came to surprises.

"Well, seeing as you brought up the subject of moving…" Lance let his voice trail off, and she just knew that she was in for another lecture. He shrugged his indifference to her annoyance and fell into step by her side as she crossed the gravel drive to the wraparound porch. "Would it really be so bad to stay with Dad a bit longer than you'd planned? I know it goes against those lists of yours, but it's not like your place doesn't need a little bit more work before you need to move in. Why not wait another week?"

Gwen didn't want their dad to overhear the upcoming conversation, especially when she got to the part where she was just as capable to taking care of herself as her brothers were. They seemed to forget that she served her country and had the means and capability of defending herself, if the need ever arose.

The heavy sweater she'd chosen to wear today wasn't enough to keep the chill at bay indefinitely, but she wasn't about to head inside for a jacket. She wanted this discussion over and done with.

"Did you, Noah, or Jace wait another week to move in when shit started happening at your places? I didn't think so. I've waited longer than any of you combined, so I don't want to hear any more lip from you."

"Well, we also didn't have that fucker basically painting a bullseye on our back," Lance countered wryly. He took a seat opposite her in one of the porch chairs that was able to lean back. "We're worried about you, sis. This guy is a killer who acts without remorse. He won't hesitate. He's as deadly as they come."

Gwen was worried, too. She was also angry. Furious would be a better adjective.

She'd been putting in long hours these past two weeks, doing her best to keep her current clients happy while marketing her services to her neighbors here in her hometown. It was hard to keep a smile on her face when she was training Beth Ann and trying to pull in new clients knowing that her name was being printed in the papers connecting her to the murder investigation.

It was bad enough that Harlan was still holding a small grudge against her after Beth Ann told him that she was quitting. He'd been a bit appeased when she'd presented him with the idea of Mindy Lipton taking over, but it was more than apparent he was still offended that she'd left him after so many years. Gwen tried to rectify the situation by buying Harlan and his wife dinner at the diner, but she still had a long road ahead to smooth over the perceived slight.

Regardless, Harlan and his wife had joined in with the rest of the townsfolk to express their concern over the latest developments and the graffiti on her barn.

"I'm not giving this psychopath the satisfaction of watching a grown-ass woman hide out at her father's house because she's too scared to live at her own damned house."

Gwen thought back to when Mitch had shown up at her new offices with Agent Thorne. She could have cut the tension with a knife, but she'd wanted to cut someone else after they'd explained the latest development.

A few days after her property had been vandalized, Charlene Winston went on the six o'clock news to let her viewers know that the serial killer had reached out to her personally. Apparently, he wanted his story told to the public at large.

To say that newspaper sales had skyrocketed was an understatement.

Mitch and Agent Thorne had both been in agreement that Charlene Winston was being conned by someone seeking attention. Their theory was that Gwen's return had somehow piqued the killer's interest since her family had become involved, and he was becoming frustrated that he couldn't reach out to her directly. It wasn't that she wasn't accessible, but rather that she was constantly in someone's presence that had the killer seeking other avenues to communicate with her.

"Agent Thorne has assigned a couple of agents to watch over me," Gwen said matter-of-factly, nodding toward the vehicle that had parked farther down the gravel driveway toward the road. "I couldn't be safer if you were in my hip pocket."

"Deputy Wallace thought he was safe because of his uniform, but we all know how that turned out." Lance used his work boot against the wooden planks to rock his chair back and forth. He was talking about the officer who'd been murdered out near Noah's place after his return to town. The consensus was the killer returned to Noah's property once Sophia Morton's body had been found inside one of the walls, not expecting to find one of the deputies at the bottom of the drive. "Bottom line? No one is safe if this scumbag was willing to kill a police officer at the drop of a hat."

Such a warning had both of them scanning the darkness that surrounded the house. Their training was hard to ignore. The crickets weren't that talkative tonight, but they weren't completely silent, either.

There was an ominous air hanging over the shadows, but not in a way that indicated an immediate threat. The sensation was that of waking up underneath a warm blanket, yet having the impression of being stifled in a way that made it hard to breathe.

This wasn't the Blyth Lake she remembered from her childhood. It had been stolen from all of them by a serial killer who wanted their attention.

"Agent Thorne's profiler doesn't seem to believe I fit this *unsub's victimology*." Grace always wondered if the feds actually used those words and spoke in such a distinct language. Turns out they did. "And technically nothing has happened since the graffiti was left on my barn."

"Technically?" Lance's steady sway had steadily increased with his irritation. "The guy is sending love notes to Charlene Winston, trying to rationalize the vandalism to your property as a way of welcoming you home. He mentioned you by name, sis. I don't think you can say nothing else has happened when it's plain as day that you are in his sights."

"Mitch's contact is looking over the information to see if she concurs with—"

"Fuck Mitch's contact," Lance blurted out, slamming the chair forward as his boots hit the porch. "She's not here on the ground, Gwen. We are sitting right here next to you, and I've been one of the hunted before. I understand when the advantage rests with the other side. None of us believe it's safe for you to move into that place where there's no—"

"The security firm all of you are currently utilizing for your own homes has already outfitted my house with a state of the art system." Gwen wasn't allowing her baby brother to railroad her with a guilt trip. "I'm not going to get into debate about the huge differences between the Navy and Marines, because we'll both end up on the ground with Dad playing referee. The point I'm trying to make is I've had self-defense training, I'm more than capable of taking care of myself against a determined adversary, and I won't hesitate to shoot a perp if I'm in fear for my life."

Lance leaned his head down and pressed the heels of his hands against his eyes, but his obvious frustration wasn't going to change her mind.

"I didn't return home to hide away in my childhood bedroom, as if I were afraid of the dark."

"Your Barbie dolls had high hopes, you know. There's a party at the dream house tonight. Ken's going to be there with GI Joe."

Gwen covered her mouth with her hand to prevent him from witnessing her smile.

Lance always did this, and she'd always end up forgetting why they were even arguing in the first place. Unfortunately, that wasn't going to happen quite so easily this time.

"What's going on with you and Schaeffer?" Lance asked after having called somewhat of a truce with his humor. She didn't doubt they would revisit the subject, but she'd learned how to stand her ground long ago. "He doesn't seem like your type."

"We're just friends," Gwen replied automatically, having said the same statement quite a few times to each of her brothers over the last two weeks. "Besides, he's younger than me."

Gwen realized her mistake the second she'd made it, but it was too late to backtrack now. Besides, she shouldn't have to make excuses. She was a grown woman, and she was free to do as she pleased. It was one of the reasons she'd originally stayed away from home, but that decision had ultimately backfired on her.

"I might have struggled with math back in elementary school, but I'm relatively sure two years difference means squat at our age." Lance lifted his right eyebrow in the same manner that Mitch did when she said something he didn't quite agree with. Damn it. Why hadn't she been given that trait? "Oh, wait. I get it. You're like one of those cougars, trolling around for those younger men."

"Mom must have dropped you on your head when you were a baby."

"I think it was Mitch, but he won't admit it."

"What does it matter if I'm friends with Chad, anyway?" Gwen never could understand why there was a double standard when it came to women being friends with men. "He's a great sounding board, doesn't judge me the way you're doing now, and he's worked twelve-hour days to make sure my house is habitable for tomorrow. Oh, and the free corn mash whiskey is a major bonus. I'm pretty sure his grandpa added molasses after he distilled it."

Gwen did her best to appear nonchalant in her description of a man she was falling for a little more each and every day. It hadn't been her intention, though the underlying physical attraction had been there from day one.

It was hard to stay immune to the casual glances, infectious smiles, and charming winks.

The thing of it was…she was relatively sure those small gestures were part of his everyday personality. He wasn't coming on to her. He was just being who he was…a decent man and better friend. She'd slowly become more attracted to him with each passing evening they spent together. How could something so innocent in the beginning burn on so steadily and actually grow into an inferno that she had no chance of extinguishing?

"Oh, shit," Lance muttered as he recognized her weakness. He'd taken in more than she would have liked, and now she had to do damage control. "You—"

"Chad has been in need of a friend, too," Gwen began to explain, not giving Lance time to say anything that would have her taking him out of that chair and begging to say uncle. "It's not what you think. Anyway, can you believe that Irish's sister was one of the victims in the lake?"

Lance fell quiet, telling her that he was debating on which discussion to continue. The town was abuzz again after reading about the letters being sent to Charlene Winston and finding out the identity of another young girl who'd lost her life too soon. It was all anyone ever talked about at the diner, The Cavern, and the hair salon.

"Irish hasn't been by the bar since Mitch and Agent Thorne notified him." Lance proved that he had a heart, not that she ever doubted it. "I was thinking of taking the truck in for an oil change just to check on him. We didn't get off to the greatest of starts."

Gwen didn't want to bring Chad into the conversation again, but it wasn't like she could separate the two friends. Irish had even joined her and Chad for a beer a couple of nights ago.

"I saw Irish on Tuesday." Gwen brushed away some of her hair that was getting in her eyes. She needed a trim on her bangs, but she couldn't bring herself to make an appointment. The forty-five minute opening for a cut and style would be spent evading one question after another about the Kendalls' involvement in the investigation. "He basically has the same story as Reese. The last place his sister had been seen was at Annie's Diner."

"I don't understand why the police never made the connection. Had someone connected the dots, maybe this scumbag would have been behind bars instead of still terrorizing our small town."

"The problem was that other sightings put her in New York City months after, though they couldn't be confirmed." Gwen thought back to her talk with Irish. "You know, he never stopped looking for her. He even hired a private detective, who was the sole reason why Irish had come to town to check out what happened to her here."

"And what?" Lance asked, not being privy to this part of the story. "Irish decided to give up his life in the city and move here? That sounds like the plot to some terrible B-rated movie."

"It's the truth. The day he arrived was the day of old man Delaney's funeral," Gwen recounted as she recalled Irish's story. "Everyone in town was talking about how the garage was for sale, and he said he took it as a sign that he should stay and get his hands dirty."

Lance once again lifted his eyebrow in that irritating manner.

"I know it sounds hokey, but think about it from Irish's standpoint." Gwen wrapped her arms around herself in an attempt to keep what body heat she could. She couldn't stay out here much longer. "We were born into a big family. Irish wasn't. Think about how we reacted to Mom's death. It brought us all home, didn't it?"

Lance didn't dispute her analogy, and it also caused him to

be silent. That was quite a feat and one she would take advantage of while she could.

"The moving company will be at the house around eight o'clock tomorrow morning," Gwen said, faking a yawn and stretching her arms above her head. She immediately regretted the action as the tentacles of cold air immediately broke through the small holes in her sweater. "Will you and Brynn be there to help?"

"Dad would kick our asses if we weren't," Lance muttered, rubbing his eyes again. "Is lover boy going to be there?"

"I'm going to take the high road and pretend that you didn't just say that."

Gwen debated adding on to that warning, saying once again that she and Chad were just friends. Protesting too much would get the wrong result, so she stood from the chair and began to walk to the front door. A quick glance down the driveway told her that one of the agents Thorne had assigned was still awake and in position.

They had to be bored as shit.

"You could do worse," Lance offered up with a shrug, still not willing to give this subject a break. "You could be *friends* with Wylie Tilmadge's son. Last I heard, Shelby was saying he had proof of his father's abduction."

"Wylie had a son named Shelby?"

Okay, that bit of news had Gwen turning before she opened the screened door. Wylie had been a conspiracy theorist who used to live on the outskirts of town, claiming that the government had been taken over by aliens. There had even been an article published in one of the local newspapers about his accounts of his own abduction.

"We've been gone a long time, sis." Lance finally stood, following her lead. He veered down the stairs before turning and walking backward toward his beat-up old truck. "Blyth Lake isn't the same town we left."

"No, it isn't," Gwen whispered, more to herself seeing as Lance was already opening the door on his F-150. "I wonder if it ever was."

There was no denying that their childhood home had been plagued with an evil unlike anything these residents had ever seen before. Gwen and her brothers had been in the pits of hell, but this was different.

This was personal, and they weren't going to take it lying down.

Chapter Thirteen

"**H**EADS UP!"

Chad caught the can of beer Noah had tossed him at chest height from about two feet in front of him, but he didn't immediately pop the tab. He took the time to wipe the sweat from his brow with the rag he'd stuffed in his back pocket. The temperature was perfect for this type of physical activity, but that didn't mean he wasn't working up a sheen of sweat from moving heavy furniture all morning.

It seemed as if the wood pieces weren't made of two-inch thick American hardwood, Gwen wasn't interested in owning it. She must go through a gallon of Murphy's Oil Soap every month. The oak two-door armoire he and Noah had just moved had to weigh at least four hundred pounds...and that was with the drawers pulled out.

Chad finally clicked the tab three times to settle the bubbles inside the can. The last two weeks working around this house had been interesting and downright vexing in unexpected ways.

Gwen wasn't anything like the young girl who'd left Blyth Lake for the Navy. She challenged him in a way no one else did, listened intently when he needed a sounding board, and shared with him stories of her own tribulations. An underlying level of trust had formed in a way that he hadn't expected, even though he'd done his best to maintain a modicum of distance. She'd drawn him in by sharing her confidence.

There was only one problem.

He now wanted more.

"Did you see this morning's paper?" Gwen had come up behind Chad and then slid around him to sit on the bare mattress he and Noah had just set on the cross-members they'd brought up with the drawers for the armoire. "Charlene Winston received another letter."

"I saw it earlier." Chad was well aware that everyone in town knew that Gwen had been spending most of her evenings at his house, though no one had said anything about their friendship to his face—not even her brothers. Chad wanted to keep it that way, so he walked over to the far wall to use as leverage while slowly pulling the tab on the beer can to ease the pressure as he opened it. "I'll swing by the garage to see how Irish is holding up. He wasn't answering my phone calls this morning."

The letter had gone in depth with regards to how the killer had saved Nora McCleary from an unhappy life. It had included details about her crying at one of the tables at the diner and how she'd poured her heart out to Annie Osburn—the owner and operator of the diner, who now happened to be retired.

Agent Thorne had been paying the older woman a lot of visits in the past two weeks, because almost every detail the killer revealed about his victims included the popular hotspot. There were other places mentioned, such as The Cavern and the lake where swimmers gathered in the summer.

It seemed that the killer had easily blended in and gone unnoticed when the town's inhabitants had traded stories of their daily lives in Blyth Lake. No one could remember a single common person at each of those locations on the days mentioned...other than those neighbors and friends who couldn't possibly be the killer.

It was as if he was invisible.

There was no doubt that Blyth Lake was home to this sick and twisted psychopath. Once again, everyone began to look at everyone else with distrust.

"Agent Thorne is pulling his agents from my detail as of this morning."

"Why the fuck would he do that?" Noah blurted out, resting against the windowsill as he took the brunt of the latest news. "Gwen, I don't think—"

"You have a bad habit of doing that," Lance said, suddenly appearing in the doorway with a smile which slowly faded when no one laughed at his jab. "What's wrong now?"

"Gwen just shared with us that Thorne is pulling her protective detail."

The two brothers began talking loud enough that it drew the others from wherever they were in the house. In under twenty seconds, everyone had gathered in the master bedroom and were talking over one another in their need to have their professional opinions heard.

The only silent ones were Chad and Gwen.

He met her gaze and gave her a small smile of support, though it wouldn't curb her reaction one bit. Her blue eyes began to darken in frustration. There she stood with a 9mm Beretta on her side, and probably four other firearms between the lot of them.

Chad figured the killer didn't have a snowball's chance in hell if that psychopath tried anything with Gwen.

She understood deep down that every single family member in this room loved her and felt the need to protect her. Yet she wouldn't allow them to dictate her actions.

The thing of it was that he cared for her, too. It had taken everything in him not to overreact to her statement about being left here by herself without armed backup within sight. He was also aware that she'd taken everyone's concern the wrong way, ignoring what her heart knew to be the truth.

He began to count silently.

Three.

Two.

One…

"Everyone stop!"

Gwen had stood up from the mattress, bringing her to stand right next to her father's side. Gus had given his opinion about Gwen remaining at his house, but he'd also been watching his daughter's reaction to the chaos. He was currently chewing on that toothpick rather intently.

"Gwen, you're being stubborn about this," Jace countered with his usual overwhelming concern, ignoring Shae's hand on his arm. It was easy to see she had on her professional hat of psychiatry, not that it would do any good in this situation. Most of the families in Blyth Lake were well beyond crazy, making them too far gone for even her services. "Your safety is more important than—"

"Let me ask you something." Gwen held up her hand when everyone tried once again to talk over one another. "I'm being serious. Every single one of us has been touched by this investigation. Noah, you and Reese found Sophia's body in one of the walls of your house. Lance, you found photographs of some of the past victims. Jace, Shae was taken by this psychopath and managed to escape by sheer determination…yet the feds don't have a detail on her anymore, either."

"Gwen is completely right," Shae said softly, coming to Gwen's defense before spinning it back to the point of this discussion. "With that said, I do take precautions. I'm sure we all do. I don't go anywhere alone or unarmed. Jace has been driving me to and from the hospital. I check my weapon at the security checkpoint on the way in and recover it on my way out. I'll call someone in the family or even have one of Mitch's deputies follow me to and from any destination outside of work."

"You also live with me," Jace pointed out in frustration as Noah backed him up, even pointing out that Shae worked in a hospital with armed security whereas Gwen's office space on Main Street was basically a high value target. "Gwen, what if you…"

Chad took another drink of his beer as the conversation ensued, nobody giving any indication that they were getting back to work anytime soon. Technically, there wasn't much left to do other than shifting a few pieces of furniture here and there to Gwen's specifications. The delivery truck had left around a half an hour ago after offloading the last of her garage items into the tool shed.

"You don't have an opinion you want to share?" Lance asked quietly, having made his way over to join Chad against the far wall. "Being Gwen's close friend and all?"

"Is there something you're trying to say, Lance?" Chad couldn't hold back his smirk, knowing exactly how the youngest of the Kendalls worked around a conversation until he got the answers he sought. It was usually done with humor, but there was nothing funny about the current situation they found themselves in. "It's not like you to hold back questions."

"I've always had respect for you, Schaeffer." This was taking a turn Chad wasn't so sure he wanted to take. He suddenly lost the taste for the beer in his hand. "Your brothers…well, not as much. I don't know what's going on between you and Gwen, but it's obvious she values your opinion."

"I'm not going to take advantage of our friendship to push your agenda, if that's what you're suggesting I do. If she wants my opinion, she'll ask for it."

"So, you think it's fine that Gwen stays here all by herself?" Lance asked, not able to keep his tone as quiet as before. Brynn's blonde ponytail swung their way. "Maybe you're not the—"

"You really don't want to go down that road, Lance," Chad warned, wishing he'd been smart enough to leave the bedroom when Gwen had dropped the news about Thorne's decision in the first place. "Gwen and I are friends. I'm not in the position to insist on anything when it comes to your sister. She's a grown woman and more than capable of making decisions on her own. I trust that she knows what she's doing and understands that I'm just a phone call away should she need my help burying the body."

"Did I miss something?" Mitch asked, appearing in the doorway much like Lance had fifteen minutes ago. Which was fourteen minutes too long to still be having this conversation. Chad was beginning to understand why Gwen had stayed away from home for so long. "From the look on Gwen's face, I'm guessing she told you about Agent Thorne's decision to pull her agents?"

A round of questions were hurled in Mitch's direction, giving Chad a breather from what could have been a very nasty confrontation with Lance. Had there been any room for Chad to make his way toward the exit, he would have done so already.

This was one of the exact reasons why he usually dated outside of Blyth Lake. Too many family connections made it hard to have a relationship without everyone having their own opinion on every damned detail. Everyone knew everyone else's business, and everyone had deeply held views on how things should progress in a proper relationship. One was lucky if the parish priest didn't weigh in on some issue or another.

Chad and Gwen had been able to keep from crossing that particular line, but it was apparent from Lance's attitude that others around town thought differently.

Maybe it was time they pulled back a little. Hell, he hadn't been to The Cavern in over a week. No wonder tongues were wagging.

"...and I don't blame him." Mitch was in the process of explaining the events that led to Thorne's decision. "Resources are limited. Thorne had a call to make, and he made it. The perp we're looking for is revealing more of himself with each letter he sends to Charlene Winston. He hasn't mentioned neither Shae nor Gwen for over a week. As a matter of fact, he seems to be more focused on that runaway from Cleveland who's made national news lately."

There was really no reason for Chad to still be in the room and involved in this family discussion. Unfortunately, Mitch brought his name up anyway.

"Chad has been making rounds on the property every morning before he begins work on the house and once again before he leaves for the night. Not once in the last two weeks has he seen anything out of the ordinary." Mitch was now leaning up against the doorframe with his arms crossed, seemingly comfortable with Gwen's decision to move in today. "I'm not saying Gwen shouldn't take precautions, but we all know that she's a hell of a lot more cautious than the rest of us. She's armed and knows how to use a weapon. She already has a state of the art security system for the house up and working. I was able to put a rush on her concealed carry permit. I'll still have Deputy Byron make his evening tour through the area. We didn't put our lives on hold for this scumbag. Neither should she. Gwen shouldn't have to accommodate our uncertainties."

The room fell quiet, telling Chad that Mitch's opinion carried a lot more weight than most. That wasn't surprising, considering he was the oldest and had taken the fundamental role as sheriff in the community.

"This is offensive," Gwen said, crossing her arms and leveling her family with a lethal stare that would have shriveled most men's balls. "Mitch speaks, so you all bow? You realize that I was going to move in here regardless of anything any of you said, right? It's not up to any of you. It's my decision."

Mitch gave one of his rare smiles, pushing off the doorframe and walking downstairs as the rest of the group followed suit, giving him shit for not arriving earlier to help move the big-ticket items that weight in over a metric ton or so. Gwen had given Chad another list of things she'd like done to the house now that the arrangements had been decided, adding to the detailed bill he'd yet to write up, much to his father's chagrin.

It wasn't like she wouldn't get the family discount already, especially considering Noah was now part of Schaeffer Contracting & Flooring.

"I didn't mean to give you shit," Lance said before Brynn grabbed his hand to join the others. "Seriously, please keep an eye out for any trouble while you're here…day or night."

Lance chuckled when Brynn gave him a little shove in response to his dig.

It wasn't long until Chad was by himself, giving him a chance to finish his beer. It was warm and didn't taste nearly as refreshing as when he'd first popped the can, but it was better than listening to her family fight.

"Hey, you."

"Hey, back." Chad was still leaning against the windowsill. He was surprised that Gwen had come back upstairs, almost wishing she'd stayed with her family below. He'd already made the decision to distance himself from her a bit more. Her seeking him out would only give Lance and the others the wrong idea about what kind of relationship they had, providing them with more fodder than they already had. "I'll start on that list you gave me first thing Monday morning. Oh, that reminds me."

Chad shifted so that he could reach in the front pocket of his jeans for his key ring. He set his empty beer can down beside him and tried to lift the metal lip in order to remove Gwen's house key.

"You'll be wanting this back now that you've moved in." Chad didn't have the nails needed to pry the ring apart, so he reached into his other pocket where he carried a small pocket-knife. "I'll make sure I'm here before you leave for work on Monday morning."

Gwen slowly crossed the bedroom floor that had turned out better than he'd expected, not stopping until she was standing inches from him. Her blue eyes weren't focused on the keyring, but rather on his lips.

Damn, if she didn't just raise the temperature in this house by twenty damn degrees.

Her lashes slowly lifted until her gaze connected with his.

"I'm tired of knocking around about this, Chad," Gwen murmured, reaching out and gently resting her hand on his. "Keep the key. You're going to need it when you come by tonight."

Chapter Fourteen

G WEN GLANCED AT the blue LED clock on the old stove that was scheduled to be replaced sometime later this week. It was going on nineteen hundred hours, and there was still no sign of Chad. She debated giving the lasagna five more minutes to give the cheese on top a chance to crisp.

"What if he doesn't show tonight?" Gwen asked herself, tossing the oven mitt on the counter. The first thing she'd done after all the furniture had been moved and arranged more times than her brothers would have liked was to unpack the kitchen boxes. A couple of loads of dishes in the dishwasher and the appliances stored away had the kitchen basically done. Apparently, for an evening alone. "You'll be eating a lot of leftovers, girl."

Gwen was never comfortable talking to herself, and she doubted that would ever change. Now that she was finally back home, maybe getting a puppy would be the way to go. After all, she was close enough to town that she could swing by home for lunch every day. And with Beth Ann being such a quick learner, Gwen might actually have an occasional day off sometime in the near future.

Another minute blinked by on the clock.

Had Chad really decided not to show? Was the pressure from her family fight earlier too much? Or was it her desire to have multiple lists and a dozen planners to show him the efficiency that could be had with the future projects she'd given

Schaeffer's Contracting & Flooring?

A few unpleasant memories from her last relationship surfaced. Rich had hated her need to plan everything down to the last detail. He'd said it ruined his need for spontaneity. It also hadn't helped that she worked fourteen hour days, leaving little to no downtime for the expensive dinners he always seemed to want to attend at various friends' flats.

City life was certainly different than country life, and she once again had to shove aside the guilt that reared its ugly head at the fact that she hadn't listened to her mother's advice about her family roots long ago.

She walked over to the fridge, grateful that Reese had offered to run to the grocery store today to buy the essentials. The woman had done that and more. Gwen wouldn't need to go shopping for another couple of weeks, with the exception of the normal staples like milk and bread.

The slight dent in the old refrigerator door drew Gwen's gaze, but it was the faint spots on the wall that the painters had missed that caught her attention the most. They couldn't be seen unless the reflection of the light hit them just so. The brightness seemed to be absorbed by the old enamel. The slap and dash job told her that Pamela Graber's parents hadn't been the ones to wield the paintbrushes. This was most likely done by the last tenants.

It wasn't that much of a concern, considering that Gwen had yet to pick her color scheme for the kitchen. Any chance of her missing a spot on the wall was highly unlikely. Her approach would provide full coverage of at least two coats' worth.

She gently ran her thumb over the faded spot.

There was another line above it, but that's when whoever was painting thickened out their strokes. It dawned on Gwen that this was where Pamela's parents had measured her growing up. The Kendalls had done the same, though each of them had chosen their own closet to keep track of their height. The wooden frame in her room back at her dad's place still had her measurements.

It must have been painful for them to leave these memories.

"Did you actually cook for me, city girl?"

Gwen would have probably screamed like a little girl at the sight of a spider bouncing on its web had she not first heard the faint sound of her cell phone chiming as the proximity alarm announced Chad's presence. The security firm who'd set up her system had the surrounding area of the house monitored for any movement. It came in handy for times like this, but for some reason, blood rushed to her cheeks and her heartbeat accelerated as if she'd just run a mile or two.

When was the last time a man affected her in such a manner?

Too long to count, which was the sole reason she'd refused to take back her key earlier this afternoon. It wasn't like they were making a serious commitment to one another, and he would ultimately need to be able to come and go while working on her house.

"City girl?" Gwen opened the fridge and pulled out two bottles of beer to give time for the flush of color to leave her face. "Since when do you consider me a city girl?"

"Well, let's see." The intoxicating scent of Chad's cologne told her that he'd moved into the kitchen and was now in close proximity. "You put in excessively long hours at your new firm, you complained that there wasn't one of those fancy coffee places in town open twenty-four hours for your convenience, and today was the first time I've seen you in a pair of jeans since last weekend. I'd say that qualifies you as more city than country."

Gwen silently handed over his beer, giving herself time to

study him before responding to such a ludicrous claim. Well, it did have *some* merit, but she'd address that at the appropriate time.

It was obvious he'd showered recently. The ends of his hair that curled slightly were still damp, and her fingers itched to brush them away from his face. He was freshly shaven with a slight sheen where he'd put on his aftershave. She fought the urge to rest her hand against his cheek. She still wasn't sure he was here for reasons other than he didn't want to stand her up on her invitation.

"I wasn't completely sure you were going to show up here tonight," Gwen finally said rather quietly.

She was unusually tentative to start this conversation considering all of this had been her idea to start with. She also wasn't usually so cautious with what she wanted.

If she wanted something, she bought it.

If she craved something, she ate it…within her own limitations.

She was a natural born go-getter, but that wasn't unusual given that she was raised with four brothers. This thing with Chad? She wasn't quite sure what tactic to take for fear that he'd want nothing to do with her or her offer for more.

"I wasn't sure, either," Chad responded honestly, the cap on his beer still secured to the opening. "I'm pretty certain Tobias was about to come out of his house to check on me when I stood by the driver's side door of my truck for ten minutes debating the idea."

Many times over the course of the past two weeks they'd had random debates over the silliest of things. She enjoyed a spirited conversation of opposing ideas and listening to his opinions, which were not much different than her own. Well, other than his preference of Dodge over Ford…which was totally insane.

"What eventually changed your mind and had you deciding to hop in that thing you call a truck and drive over here?"

"This."

Gwen wasn't expecting Chad to move in for the kill quite so quickly, but he did so with grace and lethal intent. She was a goner the moment his lips brushed over hers. The result was a foregone conclusion before she could take another breath.

Chad must have set his bottle of beer on the counter, because both of his hands were cradling her face. There was no hesitation. There was no uncertainty that he spoke of earlier, and she decided she'd have to take stock in whatever brand of aftershave he used before coming over tonight.

She was now addicted.

How could Chad Schaeffer—the skinny boy she remembered having freckles—turn into a man who could buckle her knees with a single kiss?

"Are *you* sure about this?" Chad asked, his tone a little breathless. At least he was able to talk. Her lips were still tingling, and she wasn't nearly done savoring his taste of mint mouthwash. "There's still time to—"

"*This* is exactly what I've been dying to do since I pulled up to the house and saw you standing on my porch," Gwen managed to say, setting her beer down next to his. "The only thing missing was a big red bow."

Chad lifted her underneath the arms, causing her to lose her breath at his obvious intention. She wrapped her legs around his waist and her arms around his neck, not wanting to waste any more time than they already had.

"Did you put any precautions on that list that Reese took to the store today?"

Gwen smiled against his neck, getting the gist of where this very brief conversation was headed. They wouldn't be talking for long.

"No," Gwen answered with a laugh, not expecting him to set both hands on her ass and hoist her over his shoulder. "Chad! Put me down!"

"It's a good thing they were on mine."

Chapter Fifteen

C HAD HAD STRETCHED the truth when he'd said that he stood outside of his truck for a good ten minutes. He'd spent nearly twice that standing there weighing the pros and cons of taking Gwen up on her offer. The thing about small town living was that a lot of choices made didn't affect only one person. And in their case, that was the absolute truth.

The breathtaking vision of Gwen's blue eyes staring up at him from her bed had been the catalyst.

The thing of it was that his fantasy had nothing on actual reality.

"Oh!"

Gwen dug her fingers into the pillow and let out that small exclamation when he slowly ran a hand up her inner thigh. He was positioned in between her legs, but he wasn't nearly ready to proceed without appreciating the view before him.

They'd quickly shed their clothes the moment they hit the bedroom door. Her bed had been made, but he'd quickly pulled back the country-style comforter she'd chosen as part of the rustic décor. He was a little too busy to admire what she'd accomplished since this morning.

"Chad, would you just—"

"There's that city girl shining through again," Chad teased, resting her bare foot against his chest as he pressed his lips against the sensitive part of her ankle. She was lying open to him in the most vulnerable manner, yet that vicious streak of independence shone through those baby blues of hers. There was no doubt that she was in as much control of this moment as he was, but that didn't mean he couldn't have a little fun. "Us country boys like to take our time when it comes to such things."

A bubble of laughter surfaced, but it quickly changed to a moan of pleasure when Chad reversed his touch. The closer he got to her core, the more her lips parted in anticipation…the same red lips that he'd tried his damndest to smear. He'd been unsuccessful in that endeavor, but he wasn't a quitter.

The last thing he was expecting was for Gwen to use the leverage he'd given her by placing her bare foot against his chest. She all but knocked him over backward until he was lying on his back and she was straddling him in victory.

"I'm getting a bit tired of you calling me city girl," Gwen murmured with a smile, showing him that she didn't mean a word of what she said before placing those red lips on his chest. "Let's see what this country girl remembers about country boys, shall we?"

Chad wasn't even remotely done exploring her body, but she began her descent. Her heat was like a warm blanket on a cold night. He soaked in every light touch and feathered caress.

"We like rodeos," Chad managed to remind her right before she settled herself between his legs.

Gwen didn't respond with a witty reply, but he didn't mind. She'd wrapped her hand around his cock. It was as if her hand was literally made of fire. He quickly changed his mind when she licked his tip with her tongue.

Damn.

He wasn't sure he was going to survive to give her that rodeo ride.

Every day for two weeks he'd imagined this very moment, telling himself that it would never come to fruition. A Kendall and a Schaeffer? The world must have spun backward.

Yet here he was.

Gwen drew him into her mouth, gliding those red lips over his tip and down his shaft. He couldn't drag his gaze away from the mesmerizing sight. She took him to the back of her throat at the same time she cupped his balls.

Chad closed his eyes involuntarily, which only served to heighten the overwhelming sensation of her swallowing. Her tongue pressed against his shaft and then released, starting the process all over again.

Had he really thought this moment in time had been avoidable?

"I think I'm ready for that ride," Gwen whispered longingly before reaching for the condom he'd set on the nightstand.

"You can think all you want." Chad had her flipped over onto her back by the time he was done with his sentence, but not before her fingers had closed around the square foiled package. Her laughter drifted away when his thumb skated over her hardened nipple. "Like I said, us country boys like a slow and steady ride."

Chad took his time loving her, not worried about time or outside influences. They'd both made the decision to be in this moment together, and he would savor every second of it. He didn't leave one inch of her body untouched before turning his focus on the most sensitive parts.

Gwen's breathing became a hiss of arousal when he stroked his tongue over her clit. Her fingers were buried in his hair, tightening the more he pleasured her.

There was no need for words or clever banter.

They were past that point, only existing in each other.

Chad slowly slid his middle finger inside of her, never once giving her clit a reprieve. She was saying his name over and over, but the chant became inaudible when he began to rub the pad of his finger over her sweet spot.

The exact moment he added a second finger was the instant her sheath tightened. So as not to let her lose the momentum of her release, he continued to manipulate her clit while adding pressure to that delicate area.

She cried out as the pleasure engulfed her. He began to slowly bring her down until she gradually relaxed against the comforter beneath them. Her breathing eventually evened out, and he proceeded to kiss his way up her body until he was able to reach for the condom she'd dropped on the bed.

He was grateful they'd left the bedside lamp on, but not because the golden hue made it easier to find the contraceptive package lying there on the sheets. There was nothing more beautiful than the sight of Gwen after having been pleasured.

"You promised me a ride," Gwen whispered, finally opening her eyes to reveal the satisfaction in those baby blues of hers. The gorgeous smile that graced her lips had him hardening even more. "I just need a minute to recover. That was…"

Chad had already tossed the torn foil onto the side table. She wasn't going to get her way tonight, but there was always tomorrow. He quickly and efficiently rolled the latex over his tip and down his shaft until he was covered.

"That was only a taste of what is to come," Chad promised, keeping his tone soft so as not to disturb this intimate aura that surrounded them. He was really enjoying this side of her—a woman who he'd barely scratched the surface on. "There are no rules here, Gwen. Let's enjoy the—"

"Were you going to say *ride*?" Gwen asked amusingly, wrapping her arms around his neck as he settled himself over her.

Chad took the time to brush away a few of those black strands that had gotten caught against her skin before answering. No, he hadn't been going to say the word *ride*, but it was impossible to keep from returning her smile. The only thing that could erase it was to bring up time, because she immediately withdrew into herself to ruminate in a remorse she'd created all on her own. He understood it was something she still needed to work through, but there was no room for that tonight.

"How about we just enjoy each other," Chad muttered, having gradually arched his hips until the tip of his cock was at her entrance. He ever so slowly breached her heat and didn't stop until he was fully seated inside of her. "You are so fucking tight."

Chad hadn't meant to blurt that out, but her sheath stretched around him like they'd been made for one another. She pulled her knees higher until she was able to wrap her legs around his waist. So much for thinking she'd taken all she could, because he was able to thrust a fraction deeper.

He was leveraging himself on unsteady elbows, because it was all he could do to keep from coming. Evening out his breathing helped a bit, but she had to go and ruin what little control he had.

"Chad…" He'd heard that tone before, and that was right before she came the first time. "Please. Fuck me hard."

Chad pulled out and drove back into her. She rewarded him with nails digging into his shoulder and pressing her heels into the muscles of his lower back. He didn't stop, either. He pounded into her over and over again, until they were both calling out each other's names.

Their cries of pleasure were eventually drowned out by an unexpected shrieking alarm that had both of them scrambling off the bed. This sure as hell wasn't how they'd planned the rest of their evening, but something had set off the fire alarm...or someone.

"Gwen, get outside to my truck," Chad ordered, scrambling to pull up his jeans he'd managed to grab from the floor. He wasn't sure what the hell he was going to do about the used condom, but all he could focus on was getting Gwen to safety. "Take your weapon and phone. Lock yourself in my truck and call 9—"

Gwen was laughing by the time she ran out of the room, not bothering to grab her clothes.

"What the hell is wrong with you?" Chad asked, disbelief and anger combining in a manner he'd never experienced before. He snatched his shirt off the floor and quickly followed her down the hallway. Some psychopath had set fire to the house, most likely luring them outside for some fucked up game of murder, and she was laughing? "Gwen, did you hear me? I said—"

"It's the lasagna, Chad. I left it in the oven."

Gwen had already made it down the stairs and was still laughing as she entered the smoke-filled kitchen. She waved a hand in the air, as if that useless gesture would actually clear a path for her to see the buttons on the stove. He could only stand there in disbelief as she opened the oven and pulled out a charred square of what had once been a pan of lasagna.

He remained standing in the doorway with a used condom still on his dick, his jeans unfastened, and a shirt in his hand. It took a moment for the adrenaline to leave his bloodstream, but in that time the smoke began to slowly dissipate to reveal a very naked, yet smiling, Gwen Kendall.

"Oops. I wonder how long we have before the fire department responds."

Chapter Sixteen

"I HEARD THE fire department was called out to your new place the other night, Gwen." Jeremy Bell was sitting in his usual spot at the bar. She hadn't spent much time at The Cavern, but she was now slowly acclimating to being home. Just this morning, she and Chad had breakfast at the diner before she went into work. She'd forgotten how many tongues could wag at the first sighting of a new couple in town. She couldn't get mad at Jeremy, given that anything was probably a nice diversion from being swallowed by the grief of losing his daughter. "Everything okay out your way?"

Everything was wonderful, and that was part of the problem. She was wary of how easy it had been to return to home, give or take the occurrences of guilt that popped up every now and then. She'd been prepared for the remorse of missing her mother, but she hadn't thought in a million years she'd be ready for such an intimate relationship...and with someone from her childhood to top it all off.

Gwen also didn't want to say anything that Jeremy could take the wrong way. She was still here, while his daughter had been brutally murdered.

Life wasn't fair, but Jeremy wasn't a man to be coddled, either.

"Yes," Gwen replied reluctantly, having had enough ribbing from her family who'd discovered the truth about the fire alarm through Patty. The woman worked for Mitch as a dispatcher, but she saw and heard everything from the other public services. Jeremy had probably run into her at the diner today. "A little mishap with my lasagna recipe, is all."

Her dad and Miles both coughed, not covering up those strangled laughs in the least.

She bumped her hip into her dad's stool, who ended up clearing his throat and talking about another subject that she'd rather skip over. It was hard to miss the newspaper in front of Jeremy. The front page revealed the contents of the latest letter that had been sent to Charlene Winston.

"Can you believe one of those nicknames stuck?" Gus shook his head, shifting the toothpick to the right side of his mouth. "The papers are calling him the Blyth Lake Killer. Like that's what we want our town to be remembered by. It's a damn sacrilege, is what it is."

The others gave a chorus of agreement as Gwen caught Brynn's attention. The pretty blonde made her way over, stopping to grab two bottles of beer. Chad was in the back near the dartboard, waiting for her to join him. A quick glance his way showed that he was still studying the front entrance, waiting for a specific individual who probably wasn't going to show his face this evening.

"No Irish tonight?" Brynn asked with concern once she'd reached their corner of the bar. Gwen would have thought the bar owner had telepathy, but she was only asking what was on everyone's mind. "I was hoping he'd finally come out of that apartment overtop of the garage."

"No such luck," Gwen replied with a frown. Okay, there were three topics that she didn't want to discuss. "I know Chad was hoping Irish would make an appearance, but I don't think that's going to happen anytime soon. Are we still on for our meeting Monday morning?"

"I'd say I'll bring the coffee, but word around town is that you have one of those fancy cappuccino machines at your office." Brynn winked when another round of ohs and ahs went down the occupied stools. "I'm always up for anything that has caffeine in any form."

"It wasn't me who ratted you out. It was Beth Ann." Lance had come up behind Brynn and wrapped his arms around her waist. He pulled her back against him so that he could kiss her cheek. "Are you trying to get me in trouble?"

"You do that all on your own," Brynn said with a laugh, untangling herself and leaving him to fend for himself.

"How is Beth Ann working out for you?" Calvin asked, leaning forward so that Gwen could hear him over the music. "Is Harlan speaking to you yet?"

Gwen grabbed the two bottles of beer. It was then she realized there was something she could do that could possibly cut the tension between her and Harlan.

"Lance, could you have Brynn give Harlan's table a round of shots?"

"Now you're speaking their language," Lance said, rubbing his hands together in glee. "See, Dad? It didn't take her long to adjust back to our way of communicating."

Gwen carefully made her way through the crowd back to where Chad was waiting for her at one of the high-top tables. She was actually taken aback at the restraint her brothers had shown once she'd casually mentioned that she was having dinner with Chad—and not in the friend zone, either.

Lance hadn't done his usual *I told you so* dance, and Noah had only nodded his approval. Jace had been a little reserved in his own way, but it was Mitch whose reaction had surprised her the most. He'd appeared somewhat relieved, which told her that he was more concerned about the current events than he let on even to his own family. But that was Mitch—shouldering all the worries so that the others didn't have to. He'd been like that his entire life.

Looking back on her homecoming, it hadn't gone quite as expected. She wasn't sure why she'd thought it would be different, other than their mother not being at the center of their circle. She couldn't ignore what had been right in front of her for the last three weeks—they'd all grown up.

The Kendall siblings weren't children anymore. They'd moved away, matured, and then come back home to complete the cycle of life.

"What's the sad smile for?" Chad asked, taking both bottles from her to set them on the table. He pulled back her stool, letting her get settled before using one arm to tuck her back in. Never once did he take his eyes off her until she reassured him that all was well. "Everything okay, city girl?"

Gwen still experienced a wave of arousal every time he called her by that nickname. Memories of the first night they made love resurfaced, having her wish they were back at her place now. His house was closer, though.

"What was the reason we came out tonight?"

Chad leaned into her until his warm breath caressed her ear, preventing her from suggesting they should head to his house sooner rather than later.

"I don't want your brothers thinking I've got you handcuffed to my bed," Chad murmured, only pulling back slowly once he nipped her earlobe. To anyone looking on, he'd only kissed her cheek in a gentlemanly fashion. "Spill. What happened while you were at the bar?"

"According to Lance, I'm adapting to my roots. *Nesting* is generally the accepted term these days," Gwen replied wryly, resting her hand on top of his. She squeezed gently, letting him know that she was okay to stay awhile. How could she explain her realization without sounding foolish? "I'm accepting the fact that my brothers aren't always going to be those annoying boys they were back when we were growing up. And they all seem fine with…things."

"Being in our thirties tends to mellow us out. Like a glass of fine blended whiskey." Chad palmed his beer, but he didn't take a sip of the cool beverage. He did flash a smile, though. "This is good news for both of us. It means that I don't have to avoid Noah this week."

"Don't get me wrong," Gwen warned, wishing she could lift her right eyebrow the way her brothers did so with ease. "All four of them still have a distinct tendency to annoy me. Lance, especially. Noah might be fine with—"

"Gwen?"

She really should be paying more attention to her surroundings. Maybe it was because of the country music coming out of the jukebox or everyone talking over the other in an attempt to be heard, but Harlan had managed to come up to the high-top table without her noticing.

"Harlan," Gwen greeted, not sure if her peace offering had done its job properly. She studied the older man, noting the changes in his appearance from the time when she was a teenager just getting ready to leave for boot camp. "How are you and yours?"

"Good." Harlan nodded his head numerous times to make his point. "We're doing good. Would be doing better had you not stolen Beth Ann out from under me."

Okay, so maybe the round of shots hadn't achieved its purposes completely.

Chad moved his hand from underneath hers before leaning

his arm on the back of her high-top chair. His reassuring touch on her back let her know that she wasn't alone.

"Harlan, I didn't seek Beth Ann out. As a matter of fact, she wasn't even on my list of possible candidates to interview. She must have overheard that I was looking to fill the position and showed up on the day in question." Gwen didn't have to point out that all anyone had to do was eat a meal at the diner to know the day's gossip. "If it helps plead my case, I originally told Beth Ann that it wasn't a good idea and that she should talk to you."

"Let me guess," Harlan said, tipping back on what looked to be new cowboy boots. "Beth Ann told you that she had it all worked out."

Gwen couldn't argue that point, so she nodded her agreement. She gave Chad a quick glance to see if he was following along with the conversation, because he was being awfully quiet. He seemed as if he was only half-listening, because his gaze was steady on the front door.

Unfortunately, the new arrival wasn't the man he'd been waiting on.

Chad refocused his attention on Harlan, but he wasn't the only one taking in the overdue discussion. Gwen's distraction had let her see that Harlan's table—which included his wife, Chester and Stella, and Tiny and Rose—all raised their shot glasses when she'd peered around the town's realtor.

"Is Mindy not working out?" Gwen had almost been afraid to ask, but she and Harlan might as well put everything on the table. "Beth Ann assured me that—"

"Gwen Kendall, I'm just giving you a hard time. Mindy is doing fine." Harlan tipped back his head and gave a hearty laugh, giving the signal to everyone that bygones were bygones. He motioned for her to stand up, embracing her in a bear hug. Amazingly, he still wore the same Old Stetson cologne she remembered from so long ago. Lord knows how the company managed to stay in business all these years. "I'll admit to being a bit peeved that Beth Ann wanted to leave me, but I also understood why. It was sweet of her to go the extra lengths to ensure my day-to-day business wasn't affected. Did you know that she still stops in at the office every day on her lunch break to make sure that we don't need anything? You have a time-tested winner there, Gwen, and don't you forget come Christmas bonus time."

Gwen stepped back, catching Lance giving her a thumbs up at the way this evening had played out. Honestly, she should have come into The Cavern weeks ago. It had been her own way of integrating back into the small-town life, so maybe Chad had been right about having a little bit of city left in her.

"How's business?" Gwen settled back into her seat, now able to make some small talk and get caught up on something other than what was making headlines in the paper. "It seems as if my dad kept you rather busy there for a while."

"You didn't hear?" Harlan gave Gus a wave, knowing full well that the entire line of those sitting at the bar were staring their way. "Gus is paying for our next vacation down to Florida."

"That isn't much of a surprise, Harlan."

"You didn't hear this from me, but your dad's business was what kept me afloat recently." Harlan's smile eventually faded to an odd look of concern, and Gwen had a feeling that those headlines she'd been trying to avoid weren't being pushed aside. "Well, until this past month, that is. We've had a large number of sales around the lake, all from the same corporation. It's odd considering the market is so slow. I'm sure you can imagine that houses here in town aren't quite selling so well with that monster on the loose. Sure, the town itself is doing pretty good with all those reporters sniffing around and paying tourist prices at the few accommodations we have open this time of year. No one wants to come live in a place where young women are being abducted, killed, and dumped in the lake for the fish to—"

"We get it, Harlan," Chad intervened gently, not really wanting to hear the end of Harlan's description. The man was worked up, and rightly so. "It hasn't been easy, and this town won't be the same until this lunatic is caught. Hell, I'm not sure it will ever be the same if one company owns half the properties around the lake. Odd thing is that most of them aren't even connected properties, from what I've heard. And you know that Rose and Tiny won't sell any of the land or cottages they've got."

"It does make you wonder, though." Harlan leaned forward to rest his forearms on the high-top table. The fact that he was acting as if he were sharing a secret told Gwen that this wasn't something the locals didn't already know. "Have you two heard the latest? I'm sure you have with Mitch being the sheriff and all."

Gwen had been uneasy all evening, and she'd chalked it up to Chad's concern over Irish. He'd promised them that he'd stop in for a beer tonight, but he'd been keeping to himself ever since he'd revealed his past.

"Have we heard what, Harlan?" Gwen reluctantly asked as the tension in the air slowly began to rise. Chad's fingers had abruptly stopped moving against her back, letting her know that he was steeling himself for what was to come.

"Rumor has it that one of the unidentified victims might be Pamela Graber. You know, the same Grabers whose house you live in now."

Chapter Seventeen

G WEN HAD TO have heard wrong, because Pamela Graber hadn't even been living in Blyth Lake when Emma Irwin had been abducted. Besides, the Grabers would have said something to someone in town if their only daughter had gone missing. Nothing of that magnitude could happen without someone noticing.

"Pam went to college down south two years before I graduated high school," Chad said skeptically, dropping his arm from the back of Gwen's chair as he shifted forward. "How could she be one of the victims? Wouldn't the Grabers have said something to someone back here that their daughter had been abducted?"

Gwen thought back to the first day she'd toured her new home. She hadn't gone down to the basement until her brothers had been on hand. Had she known deep down inside that something terrible had happened to someone who had lived there?

"That's something you'll have to ask Mitch," Harlan suggested, although his words were mostly directed toward Gwen. She hadn't realized that she hadn't taken a breath until she grasped that Harlan was waiting for her to speak. "I'm sure we'll hear one way or another fairly soon. I saw that Agent Thorne walking into the police station after I had dinner over at the diner this evening."

Patty must have said something in passing about today's events, because Gwen was relatively sure that no one in her family had been made aware that Pamela could be one of the bodies discovered in the lake. Gwen had found it odd that her older brother had yet to make an appearance here at The Cavern, but he *was* the sheriff. Somebody could have had their boat stolen or something equally benign. He was technically on call twenty-four seven, but now they'd been made aware of the truth.

Harlan's recap of events still didn't make any sense.

"Chad's right," Gwen interjected, pushing her beer to the side as she rested her forearms on the table. Her heartrate had spiked, and her palms were now coated with perspiration. She couldn't be living in a house that was connected to that...monster, as Harlan so eloquently put it. "Pamela left for college the same year that I joined the military. And last I heard, she was still living somewhere down south."

"I'm just sharing what I was told earlier." Harlan patted Gwen on the shoulder in sympathy. "Thanks for the shots. And no hard feelings about Beth Ann. It's not like the pool of available talent around here is bottomless."

Gwen and Chad didn't say a word as they both watched Harlan walk back to his table. The others were looking curiously on, most likely trying to figure out where the conversation had taken a turn from looking at their expressions.

"I know what you're thinking, but I'm sure that Mitch is ruling it out as we speak. Harlan must have misunderstood whoever he was talking to earlier today."

"Chad, you and I both know that it was probably Patty speaking out of turn. And that's surprising, given that she usually never discusses cases unless it's already been verified. She wouldn't have let something like that slip if there wasn't some truth to it." A wave of nausea rolled over Gwen as she tried to slow down her thoughts. "What if Pamela was taken from—"

"The Grabers would have called the police first thing, and you know it."

It *was* unthinkable that someone from this small town, even if he or she were away at college, had met a tragic end without anyone knowing. Had Pamela been taken from her childhood home? Had the Grabers called the police? Had the former sheriff determined that there was no reason to cry foul play?

Frank Percy had been running things back then. He didn't have the best reputation for getting the job done, and that was one of the reasons Mitch had taken the so-called temporary position until a new election could be scheduled.

"What's going on?" Lance had begun his trek from behind the bar to their table the moment Harlan had left to join his group. Her brother rested his palms on the table as he waited for an answer. "You're as white as that napkin, sis."

"Harlan just shared that Pamela Graber might have been identified as one of the victims found at the bottom of the lake," Chad shared, rubbing the back of his neck in frustration. "I can't wrap my head around that possibility."

"How is that even possible?" Lance pulled his cell phone out of his front pocket, immediately pressing the home button to get to his screen. "Pam Graber left town after high school and still lives somewhere down south. Her parents moved away around three years later to be closer to her once they realized she'd most likely stay in Alabama after graduating college."

"That's what we thought," Gwen replied softly, a dead weight having settled in her stomach. What if that welcome home message hadn't been for her? What if Pam's killer had returned to the house as some kind of sick reunion now that the girl's body had been found? Gwen wasn't sure she should be relieved or worried. "Do you know anyone who kept in touch with the Grabers after they moved?"

"Rose," both Chad and Lance said in unison.

All of them glanced over at Harlan's table where the three couples sat.

"My bet is that she's already placed a call into Shelly Graber." Chad gradually sat back in his chair, though it was clear that he was still bothered by this latest development. "Gwen, I know you're not going to want to hear this, but—"

"Don't go there," Gwen warned, not planning on leaving her new home because of some idle speculation. "We'll wait to see what Mitch has to say before—"

Lance had to go and ruin her hope that this was all a misunderstanding. Her baby brother held up his phone as proof.

"Noah and Reese are at the station now. Agent Thorne just issued a press release, and Charlene Winston is doing a live telecast in front of the station as we speak."

Quite a few cell phones began to chime throughout the bar, not so much evident by the sounds as it was noticeable when the displays lit up like fireflies. Within seconds, the patrons turned to Brynn and urged her to turn on the large screen television in the corner usually reserved for Thursday night football games.

"Are you in the mood for a sleepover?" Gwen asked Chad, trying to keep things light and failing miserably.

"I thought you'd never ask," Chad responded with a small smile, allowing her to get away with keeping this a date night instead of what it truly was—another night where the citizens of Blyth Lake were on edge because of some twisted psychopath.

"HEY, CITY GIRL." Chad purposefully kept his voice low so as not to startle Gwen. Their night out hadn't been what either of them had hoped for. Finding her staring out of her living room window with a cup of coffee in her hand at three o'clock in the morning rather solidified that fact. "Your bed is getting rather cold without you in it."

"I left you in there to keep it warm." Gwen rested her head back against his shoulder when he wrapped his arms around her waist. He pressed his cheek against her hair, breathing in her intoxicating scent. He still wasn't sure how they'd ended up here together, but he'd learned not to question life when the goose handed him a golden egg. "Thanks for spending the night here."

"You have clean sheets and are pleasant company. It's a win-win for me. Someone's keeping me so distracted lately that I haven't had time to do laundry."

"Does that mean soon you'll be running around my house naked?"

Chad hadn't meant to pause the banter, but he'd almost mentioned that wasn't a possibility given the circumstances. He'd even put on his jeans after they'd made love earlier, because there was no way in hell he was being caught unaware should she receive another visit from that psycho scumbag.

"I can't believe Pamela went missing all those years ago and her parents never said a word to anyone," Gwen whispered, resting her left arm over his as they both continued to stare out the window. "Isn't that what friends are for? To confide in? To be a shoulder to cry on?"

Chad couldn't give her the answers she sought. He found his gaze inadvertently following the length of the fence around the barn and studying the shadows of the corral. Agent Thorne hadn't felt it necessary to put another detail on Gwen or Shae, but that hadn't stopped Mitch from having a couple of his deputies drive through specific areas throughout the night keeping a close eye on things.

Pamela *had* been one of the two unidentified bodies found in the lake.

From what Agent Thorne had included in the press release, Pamela Graber had gotten involved in drugs and alcohol to such an extent that her parents thought it would be beneficial to be nearby. That hadn't been the case. They'd purchased a home near the campus, all but forcing Pamela to move in with them for her last year of college.

It had come to light that Pamela and her parents had gotten into a rather heated argument in her last semester, with the young girl storming out of the house and yelling profanities. Neighbors recalled that threats of leaving and never returning had been said.

The Grabers hadn't been surprised when a couple of days passed without hearing from her. Though Craig and Shelly Graber eventually called the police, the investigation came to a halt when law enforcement gathered that Pamela Graber had left on her own free will.

"Why wouldn't Craig or Shelly have said something when Sophia Morton's body was found? They would have heard the news through friends." It was clear that the coffee Gwen was drinking had kicked in. "I mean, it was national news. So was the fact that the killer had used the lake as his own killing ground."

"Gwen, we could run in circles with this discussion until morning. We're still not going to have answers. It sounds like the Grabers were ashamed of what had transpired with their daughter. We don't know what they went through, just as they most likely never thought the crimes committed here had anything to do with events that happened there in Alabama."

"But Craig and Shelly would have known about Emma Irwin's disappearance. They were still in Blyth Lake at the time. Why wouldn't they have—"

"It sounds like Pamela had taken a very dark path, and her parents thought their presence would shed a little light on her future plans. In the end, maybe they thought they'd exposed a little too much and their good intentions backfired. We just don't know. Look, you're having Sunday dinner with your family tomorrow night. Well, technically tonight," Chad said, referring to the fact that it was three o'clock in the morning. "You'll get more answers. After all, I'm sure Mitch is looking forward to being interrogated by all of you."

Chad earned a point in the distraction arena when Gwen almost spit out her coffee. It was a reminder that she'd had enough, so he gently took it from her fingers and set the mug down on the windowsill.

"It's the truth, isn't it?" Chad asked, taking her free arm and tucking it in between his. He held her tight as they continued to stare out onto her property as it was cast in a soft moonlight glow. It was easy to see that the grass had a light frost over the blades from the way they glistened in the bluish beams. "If it weren't for your dad, I'd bet a hundred bucks that Mitch would bail on family dinner."

"Why don't you see for yourself?"

It took a few seconds for Chad to register the significance of what she was asking. It didn't take a genius to know that he had to tread carefully in the waters she'd just mucked up. Mitch wasn't the only man who didn't want to face the firing squad. He almost gave the standard excuse that he'd let his errands build up, but he could literally feel her body tighten as she prepared herself for his negative response.

"How about I swing by for dessert?"

Chad labored his breathing, waiting for some type of response.

Three weeks. Gwen had been back in town for three weeks.

Two of those were spent getting to know one another and all but going about their daily lives as if their evening talks were nothing more than a pleasant way to pass the time.

They'd been fooling themselves.

Who would have thought that two teenagers who used to run in different circles, if that was even possible in such a small town, would find themselves involved in such a short time?

"You don't like grilled steaks?"

Chad had to smile as he tucked her in closer when she would have turned around to face him. Between her lists and her penchant for schedules, it didn't surprise him that she was pushing the issue. Last Sunday, she'd even itemized each dish her brothers and significant others would be bringing in order to take the burden off their father.

What had Noah said the other day up at the lake when Chad had stopped in to check on the cottages?

Gwen would have made one hell of a drill instructor.

"How about I take a raincheck for those steaks and you save me a piece of that apple pie you're making in the morning?"

"How did you know I was making apple pie?"

"Oh, maybe it has something to do with the grocery list hanging up in the kitchen."

This time, there was no stopping Gwen from turning around in his arms. He was still wearing his jeans, but she must have picked up his flannel shirt from the other pile of clothes he'd left on the floor. Her black hair was a bit mussed, and he'd successfully succeeded in smearing that red lipstick off her lips.

"Why dessert? Why not dinner?" There was enough moonlight shining through the now spotless window thanks to the cleaning crew she'd had come in to make the house move-in ready that he could make out her blue eyes without any trouble. He'd hurt her with his response. "Is it Lance? Did he say something to you?"

"I can handle Lance if it comes to that," Chad responded with a chuckle, tucking some strands of her soft hair behind her ear. His smile faded when unpleasant memories of his childhood began to surface. "Gwen, my not being able to join you tomorrow has nothing to do with your brothers. Tomorrow marks the day we lost my mother in that car accident. I'm meeting my dad and brothers out at the cemetery, and then we're going into the city to her favorite restaurant to have a meal in her honor. It's something we used to do every year."

"Until Clayton and Wes left town," Gwen surmised, her brows furrowing as she rested the palms of her hands against his chest. It was easy to see she was searching for the right words where none were needed. Yes, he and his brothers had lost their mother. His father had lost his wife, never to remarry. But they'd survived. They'd had each other. Well, they used to have one another until his brothers up and left their family roots. "Is there anything I can do?"

"Gwen, my mom passed when I was just a boy. I grew up only knowing my dad and brothers as my family. The only sadness that remains is for a picture of a beautiful mother who was taken far too soon." Chad pulled Gwen close, pressing her cheek over his heart. The pain and sorrow she experienced in losing her own mother was vastly different than his experience, though that wasn't to say there hadn't been a missing piece in his life. "My father asked that we resume our annual commemoration now that things are somewhat getting back to the way it used to be."

"And Clayton? Will he be there?"

"Wes has promised me that he'll get Clayton to come to the cemetery tomorrow." Chad wouldn't place any bets on that, but it was nice to see Wes try to atone for being absent over these last few years. "It's important to my father that we all be together like we used to be."

"I'll save you a piece of apple pie," Gwen whispered, lowering her hands until she was able to wrap her arms around his waist. "The largest one, too. Lance will never know the difference."

"You're determined for him not to like me at all, aren't you?"

"Oh, don't let him fool you. He's always liked you. Clayton, on the other hand…"

Chad couldn't believe they were standing in her living room at three o'clock in the morning and joking about the fact that his older brother had all but tried to burn Lance's home to the ground. There was nothing humorous about having a family member of Clay's ilk.

"I suppose it could have been worse. At least he was too drunk to finish what he had gotten himself into."

They understood that the chances of both of them personally knowing the individual responsible for such heinous crimes against those young women were substantially high. It made him physically sick to his stomach that someone they trusted could kill another human being.

"Don't say that," Gwen said, tightening her arms around him as if that would keep the evil at bay. Unfortunately, it had all but saturated this town…this house included. "I don't want to believe that anyone we know could do something like that."

Unfortunately, Chad couldn't reassure her differently.

Yes, there were a few victims who hadn't been from Blyth Lake. The majority of the young girls were, though, and that was why the feds had all but descended on the town. Agent Thorne had brought in a team this evening that had basically taken over the sheriff's office. It was now only a matter of time before this nightmare was brought to its inevitable end.

He hoped like hell that all of those closest to them were still standing when it was over.

Chapter Eighteen

G WEN TURNED HER head into the soft pillow to avoid the sunlight shining in through the bedroom window. The rays were nothing but a ruse, because she'd seen the frost start to cover the lawn earlier in the morning hours before dawn. It was cold outside of this warm cocoon she found herself in, and she was going to extend the morning for as long as she could.

Entertaining the idea of decorating for the coming Halloween holiday, she made a mental note to pick up some decorations for the office. She reminisced of walking down Main Street as a child and seeing all the storefronts decorated for each of the holidays, but Halloween had always been one of her very favorites.

The flutter of the comforter broke through the barrier of her morning dream, allowing the chilly morning air to brush over her body. She should have turned the heat on last night, but she'd gotten distracted by...

"You better have my coffee with you," Gwen warned, her morning voice cracking as her words turned into a throaty laugh.

"You don't need coffee this morning." Chad's warm lips settled around her nipple, but it was the heat of his tongue that had her arching her back for more. She immediately reached for him, slipping her fingers into his hair to gain some leverage. He was a very talented man. "See? I'm pretty sure that woke you right up."

"What else do you have in your arsenal?" Gwen whispered, letting the sheet slide off them, no longer needing the blankets. He was all the heat she needed. He pressed light kisses down her abdomen until she had no choice but to spread her legs so he had the room to do his best—which usually resulted in her screaming out his name. "Oh!"

Chad had taken his tongue and slowly licked her clit until she dug her heels into the mattress. She finally relaxed somewhat when he began to nibble on the sensitive skin of her inner thigh, giving her a chance to catch her breath and enjoy his way of waking her up on a Sunday morning.

"Have you started a list of sexual positions yet?"

Gwen didn't get a chance to answer him, because he went back to paying attention to her clitoris. He gently suckled the engorged nub until she was pretty sure there were lights flashing behind her eyelids, seemingly in no hurry to have an answer. The pressure for that ultimate release began to grow as he started to draw circles with his tongue, every full loop covering every square inch of those exposed nerves.

She was right there.

Right on the edge.

That explosion of pleasure was hers for the taking.

One more stroke…

And then he stopped.

"The position we used in the bathroom was rather interesting," Chad murmured as he began his way back up to kiss her on the lips. She had enough pent-up energy to light up the entire town of Blyth Lake, and he wanted to talk about sex positions? Her brain was having trouble interpreting his words. "I don't believe I've taken you from behind yet."

Gwen didn't care how he took her, as long as he did so soon.

"You know, the experts say that a woman feels more of a

man that way," Chad murmured, slowing turning her over. They'd lost the covers long ago. There was something damn sexy about a man placing his lips in the middle of a woman's back. "Shall we find out?"

Gwen wanted to reply that they'd both tried many things in their pasts, but there was no point in bringing up other people. This was their time. Theirs alone. And she wouldn't tarnish that for anything in the world.

"I'd love to," Gwen replied readily, not caring that overwhelming need seeped through her words. She peered over her shoulder. He hadn't shaved since Friday, so a five o'clock shadow had formed long ago. It scratched her skin, but in the most provocative manner that aroused her more than she'd thought possible. "What are you waiting for, Schaeffer?"

His dark eyes became hooded at her directive, but she quickly came to realize the reason why. She'd done the same thing on the night the killer had spray-painted graffiti on the barn. It had been a way to keep him at a distance…and he'd known that.

"When I give you your release, Gwen, it's my first name you'll be calling out," Chad promised, nipping her earlobe to let her know he was serious. "No other name but my own."

Gwen wasn't sure when he'd rolled a condom over his cock, but she was very grateful that he'd had the fortitude to think ahead.

In seconds, he had her on her knees and had claimed her in one massive thrust.

She parted her lips in a silent scream of pleasure, but there was no oxygen left in her lungs to make such a sound. Every nerve in her body had been awakened, and he'd just amplified the one that would have her following his every directive.

Chad's calloused fingers took a hold of her shoulder, while his other hand firmly grasped her hip. He'd spread her legs at just the right position that she could only accept what he gave her, and she gladly took it.

Gwen had to bite her lip when he began to pull back out, the loss of fulfillment almost too much to bear.

He didn't make her wait for long.

Chad slammed back into her, his grip tightening and taking control. Over and over, he pummeled into her until he finally got what he wanted—his name falling off her lips.

Chapter Nineteen

"**I**'M SURPRISED YOU made it."

Gwen stepped out onto the front of the wraparound porch with two cups of coffee. She used her elbow to ease the screen door shut. It seemed that Dad had unhooked the chain for some reason. That was something she'd have to remedy before turning in for the night.

Usually, she'd have two sweet iced teas in hand, but a cold front had definitely moved into the area. The trick and treaters were going to have to bundle up this coming Wednesday if they wanted to earn their rewards for dressing up and navigating the neighborhoods.

"Believe it or not, I'm finding Sunday dinner with this crew easier to deal with than Agent Thorne and his group of merry men." Mitch gratefully took one of the mugs from her, though he didn't sit back in the cushioned chair. He balanced his cup of coffee on the railing and walked over to the screened door. He pulled it open and reattached the chain to its hook on the inside corner. After exchanging a knowing smile with her, he recovered his steaming beverage and reclaimed his seat before resting his elbows on his knees, almost as if he were ready to leave at a moment's notice. "I'm pretty sure Patty is ready to hand in her resignation after the day she had today."

"I'm surprised you didn't already ask for it. She dropped the ball big time." Gwen had seen her older brother in his element a time or two. He wasn't one to be messed with, and Patty was going to learn that small towns and personal relationships didn't excuse talking out of turn. A small part of Gwen felt a bit bad for the reaming the dispatcher must have endured after Mitch discovered she'd let the townsfolk know about Pamela Graber's terrible fate. "You realize she probably gets pummeled with questions on a daily basis. I wonder what she'll do next time she's put to the test."

"There's no excuse, Gwen, and you and I both know it."

"I heard that Agent Thorne was going to question everyone again in connection with Emma Irwin's abduction." Gwen didn't want to get into a debate over small town behaviors. Technically, she agreed that the way the investigation was being conducted needed to change in order to bring this killer to justice. "I heard that Uncle Jimmy is on that list, too."

Gwen took the seat next to Mitch instead of the one across from him. Chad had promised to stop at the house for the biggest piece of apple pie she'd saved for him. She was hoping to see the headlights of his truck through the pine trees at any moment. In the meantime, she might as well bring up the black sheep in the family. Chad certainly didn't get to call dibs on that one.

Gwen reached into the pocket of the lightweight jacket that belonged to her dad. She'd grabbed it from the coatrack next to the front door when she came out. The heavy turtleneck sweater wasn't nearly enough to shield her from the chill in the air.

She pressed the home button, reading the time.

Chad was late.

Really late.

"Thorne wants to bring Jimmy in to follow up his past twenty statements," Mitch said wryly, clearly believing that the federal agent was wasting his time. "His team went around knocking on doors today. That didn't go over very well amongst my potential supporters."

Gwen could sense that Mitch wasn't telling her everything. She would have left well enough alone, but now she understood why Harlan would go searching for answers. It wasn't nice being the last to know.

"Did Agent Thorne mention Chad again?" Gwen and Chad hadn't left her place until after three o'clock in the afternoon. If he'd been ambushed at his house by a team of federal agents, he might not have been given a chance to call her. "Mitch, tell me now if—"

"Thorne went into the city to speak with Clayton. The other three were basically chasing ghosts all day, considering that most of the residents were in church and then eating at the diner. They sure as hell don't know how to navigate a small town like this. Look, that's all I know right now. They aren't exactly asking my permission. I'll be heading back to the station to see if any developments occurred within the last couple of hours." Mitch took a drink of the coffee she'd brought him, staring at her as she tried to reach Chad by phone. "Is this a short-term thing you've got going on with Schaeffer?"

The call went straight to Chad's voicemail.

Gwen didn't respond to Mitch's question. She lowered her phone, taking time to gather her thoughts as she cut the connection. One, she wasn't going to overreact to the fact that Chad wasn't answering her calls. Two, Irish would have reached out to her if there was a situation. And three, she didn't have an answer for her brother one way or the other.

"I'm not asking for you to solve world hunger, sis." Mitch hid a smile behind his coffee cup. "I just didn't know if I should deal Chad into the poker game I'm hosting next week."

"And why do you get to host the first one?" Gwen asked,

buying herself some time to decide if Chad was ready to be thrown to the wolves. "It was Lance's idea to have a monthly game of dealer's choice."

"I actually wanted to take your money on a weekly basis, but Brynn said I was being too greedy with members of the family," Lance called out, holding the screen door open for Brynn. She was shaking her head, indicating she hadn't said anything of the sort. "I'll bring the chips."

"You can bring the beer, cheapskate," Noah chimed in. He and Reese were right behind the other couple. "You're such a cheap bastard. One bag of chips isn't enough for nine people, but I sure as hell know you won't skimp on the beer."

"Don't worry. I'll be in charge of the chips from now on," Brynn promised, holding up her hands to signify that she had nothing to do with Lance's bad behavior. "I gave him one job, guys. One job, and he screwed the pooch."

"That's the problem, Brynn." Jace waited for Noah to move aside, taking over door duty as Shae walked out with the crockpot she'd used to bring the baked beans. Jace had given her their mother's recipe, and Shae had perfected it to a tee. "You gave Lance a job that actually needed to be done. He does better with things much less important."

"Why am I the target tonight?" Lance complained, wrapping his arms around Brynn and swinging her off the last step of the porch. "You started this, blondie. I should make you ride home in the bed of the truck."

"Then you'd be sleeping outside on the porch, now wouldn't you?"

Gwen lifted a hand and waved as each of her brothers and significant others slowly made their way to their vehicles. Mitch drained his coffee and stood, checking his phone for any updates.

"Go," Gwen urged, knowing that he was most likely needed down at the station. Byron was a good deputy, but he didn't like the political relations that came in dealing with other law enforcement agencies. From what Mitch said, Byron called them *feds* to their faces. "Leave your coffee cup there. I'll take it inside when I take mine in."

"I appreciate it." Mitch didn't hesitate to set his empty mug on the railing. "Tell Dad that I—"

"You can tell me yourself." Gus shifted his toothpick, cuffing Mitch on the back in affection. "You did good work on the steaks tonight, son. Just a few more lessons and you should be just about there."

"I learned from the best." Mitch shifted so that their dad could sit down in the vacated seat. "You want to meet me for breakfast tomorrow morning? I'll spring for coffee, biscuits with sausage gravy, and a side order of bacon."

"You know where to find me, and that order sounds about right."

"Mitch," Gwen called out to her brother right before his work boot hit the bottom step. "Count Chad in for poker next week. Lance could lose a few dollars more."

The side of Mitch's mouth lifted in what could only be characterized as an *I knew it* smirk. He was smart enough not to comment one way or the other. All she and her dad could hear was the jingling of his keys as he strolled to his truck.

"You know, you could have invited Chad to dinner this evening." Gus leveled her a look that was basically filled with curiosity. "I would have wrangled your brothers in if they had gotten out of line."

"I can handle those buffoons on my own, Dad." Gwen had always gone to her mom for advice when it came to boys and eventually men as the years passed. This was…awkward. Her dad wasn't exactly someone she would normally go to with relationship questions. It was also the way things were now, so she might as well dive in feet first. *I hope you're with me, Mom.* "You'll be happy to know that I did extend the offer to Chad, but he had important plans with his family tonight."

At least, she hoped that's what Chad had been able to do. After speaking with Mitch, she wasn't so sure that was the case now.

"Good." Gus rested an elbow on the arm of the chair, turning to watch Mitch's taillights fade into the long line of pine trees. "It's good to see you settling in, pipsqueak. I wish Mitch would take a page out of your book, but I understand that he has a lot on his plate right now. Would you look at that? He left his coffee cup out here for me to take care of."

"He's putting in sixteen to eighteen-hour days," Gwen estimated, having heard Mitch talking with Jace about the man hours being put into this investigation. "Something is bound to break sooner or later."

"I just hope that it doesn't backfire on this town again." Gus shook his head at all the tragedy the residents of Blyth Lake had undergone for over the past decade. He was right, and it had to stop. "Enough talk about that. Tell me about you and Chad. He turned out to be a pretty good man, Gwen."

This was it. Did she confide in her father or did she continue to talk to air in hopes her mother was somewhere listening? Maybe it would help if Gwen stopped by the cemetery, but she wasn't ready for that type of closure.

"I didn't expect to start a relationship my first month back in town," Gwen admitted, breathing out slowly when Gus didn't comment one way or another. He just listened...the way her mom used to on these very same autumn nights. The only thing missing was the homemade hot chocolate, but coffee was a pretty good substitute. "Chad was a pleasant surprise."

"Love usually has a way about it."

"It's only been a few weeks, Dad." Gwen hadn't said any-thing about love. Her heart fluttered in response, anyway. "Chad's easy to talk to. He listens, he makes me laugh, and he doesn't make fun of my never-ending to-do lists. Well, he does. But in a cute way. That's a huge bonus in my book, Dad. He's compassionate and loyal. He has a sense of honor about him that no one can diminish. I'm rambling on, I know, but he's someone who I can admire. The point I'm trying to make is that I don't know where this is going quite yet, but I am going to enjoy the journey."

Gwen had basically quoted her mother. It brought a smile to her dad's face, and it was as if Gwen had won a gold medal.

"You haven't been by to see her."

Damn it.

Busted.

Gwen looked into the coffee cup still in her hand, not want-ing him to see how much his words affected her. She wasn't ready for this conversation. She'd rather talk about the birds and the bees than this. Hell, any other topic was more preferable than her mother's death.

"Gwen, this is what she wanted. More than anything, she wanted this family together."

If it had been anyone other than her father sitting across from her, Gwen would have left. Literally, she would have gotten into her Jeep and driven away as if no words had been uttered, but she stayed.

She couldn't just walk out on her father.

"We could have given this to her before she died, but we didn't." Gwen barely managed to get the words out before she had to cover her lips so that he didn't see her struggling to talk.

She gave herself a few seconds to regain what composure she could, clearing her throat and trying once more to convey what she'd agonized over the last three years. "I should have come home the moment my time was up in the Navy. I didn't have to stay in the city to start my business. I could have set up shop right here while spending time with her. Instead, I chose—"

"To live your own life. And there isn't a damn thing wrong with what or how you did it." Gus took his toothpick and pointed it in her direction. "Nothing made your mother happier than watching her baby girl grow up to be a successful businesswoman. Did you know that Mary went around town boasting about all your accomplishments? And don't even get me started about how she would gush about the important men you were dating—a doctor, a lawyer, and then some guy who wanted to take you to Paris for the holidays."

"That was Rich," Gwen said with a smile, though she couldn't get rid of the tears that had collected on her lower lashes. "Mom couldn't believe I'd told him no, but there was no way I could take two weeks off from work."

Her smile faded when she realized she'd used the same excuse to get out of everything.

"I should have come home, Dad."

"You did what you were supposed to do, young lady." Gus leaned forward and rested his elbows on his knees, getting wound up for a lecture. She'd witnessed this scene from her childhood more times than she could count. Hadn't Mitch been sitting in this same position earlier? Like father, like son. "You found your own path. Not your mother, me, nor your brothers. You. You found out what makes you tick, your likes and dislikes, and more importantly what makes you happy. And you brought it home with you so that you can raise the family your mother will be watching over from above, God willing."

The tears that had been stuck to her lashes finally fell. It was like a leak she couldn't turn off, no matter how hard she tried.

"Pipsqueak, don't think for a second your mother didn't want that for you. She was so proud of you, as am I." Gus used the back of his hand to wipe away his own couple of tears, but he remained focused on the sermon he was giving as he once again pointed his toothpick her way. "You don't judge a man by the actions of others, and you wouldn't have learned that had you come home a moment too soon. You and Chad…if the two of you are meant to be, you'll know. If your mother were here, she'd tell you that all roads lead to the same place—the place you're meant to be."

Gwen *was* in the place she was meant to be, and she didn't doubt that she was also with the man she was meant to share her life with right now. It was up to her to embrace what was right in front of her, and she would enjoy every second of it.

Her mother had been a very wise woman.

"Thanks, Dad. I needed this."

Gus was prevented from responding when headlights broke through the line of pine trees. She couldn't stop her smile from forming that Chad had come for the large slice of apple pie she'd set aside for him. Unfortunately, her grin slowly faded when she spotted the tow truck that belonged to Irish's garage.

Irish's unexpected visit signified that Chad's day hadn't gone as planned.

"What's wrong?" Grace asked, having made it off the porch in record time. She didn't even remember setting her coffee cup down, but it was no longer in her hands. "Irish? What happened?"

"First off, everything is fine," Irish assured her, leaving the truck door wide open. His words might say one thing, but his actions told her that he was needed elsewhere. "Chad and Miles were driving back to the Blyth Lake after they'd had dinner with Clayton and Wes, but they were run off the road by some drunken bastard who didn't even stop to make sure they were okay. Chad's truck ended up in a ravine with three flat tires, and it's a freaking Dodge to boot. The tow truck service up that way is taking their time to get there."

"Why didn't Chad just—"

"They're in that dead zone around an hour out," Irish explained, tossing a thumb over his shoulder as if she'd know the exact location he was referring to. Hell, she hadn't even owned a cell phone back in high school. She had no idea where the dead zones were located around here, but that point was moot. "Someone stopped at the scene, and Chad told him to reach out to my garage when the passerby reached the next town. I figured he wouldn't want you to worry, so I stopped here on my way out of town. Everyone knows that the Kendalls all have Sunday dinner together."

Gwen breathed an audible sigh of relief, patting her father's hand that he'd set on her shoulder in reassurance.

"Let me grab my purse. I'll go with you to meet them."

Gwen didn't even bother to turn away from Irish, because he was already shaking his head to the contrary.

"Gwen, I only have room for two people in the cab. Don't worry. I'll bring them back to town. I'll just drop Chad off at your place after making sure Miles gets home, if that's alright?"

"Yes, that's fine," Gwen replied, not really having a choice. It was a relief just knowing that Chad was okay. She could wait a bit longer to see him. "I appreciate you thinking of me, Irish. Thanks for driving out of your way to tell me."

Irish gave her a half smile before nodding a greeting Gus' way.

"No problem. See you in a bit."

Gwen and her father remained standing as Irish got back into the tow truck and continued to maneuver the small circle that would once again take him through the line of pine trees.

"Don't even think about it."

Gwen patted her father's hand once more before wrapping her arm around his waist and letting him guide her back up the porch steps.

"I could have followed behind, offering to drive Chad home while Irish did the same for Miles. After all, I'm sure Irish doesn't want to waste any more time on a Sunday night than he has to. Tomorrow morning will roll around awfully quick," Gwen protested, wincing when the lame excuse came off exactly as that. "Don't worry, Dad. I'll help you collect the coffee mugs off the porch. I'm the one who told Mitch to leave his there, by the way."

"You wanting to head back inside the house has nothing to do with grabbing that large piece of apple pie I found hidden behind the toaster, would it?"

Gwen should have known that she couldn't get anything around her father. Just as she was well aware that he could sense the concern she was still experiencing over Irish's visit. He'd mentioned that the individual responsible for running Chad and Miles off the road was probably inebriated and didn't even realize what had happened.

But what if that wasn't the case?

What if it was something else altogether?

Gwen didn't consider herself one of those people who over-reacted at the slightest of things, but something was wrong with this picture.

It wasn't like she could do anything about it right now, and Chad and Miles were patiently waiting for Irish to come and pick them up. The least she could do was to have a piece of warm apple pie with vanilla ice cream on the side waiting for Chad when he finally came home.

"Dad, do you have any of that homemade vanilla ice cream left from last Sunday?"

Chapter Twenty

"**I** APPRECIATE THIS," Chad said for the fifth time in the last twenty minutes. That's how long it had taken Irish to pull the damaged truck out of the ravine after the first wrecker service had failed in two prolonged attempts. The different approach utilized by Irish was successful when he used the spare on the truck to replace the one rim that was damaged. He was able to inflate two of the other tires to make recovery much easier. "I know that was a long drive, but I don't trust anyone else to handle my baby."

"Your baby was at her father's house," Irish quipped, wiping his hands on the rag he usually kept in the back pocket of his worn jeans. He'd taken off the light jacket he had on when he'd arrived within minutes of viewing the scene before him. "And let me tell you something. I'm surprised her headlights weren't attached to my bumper all the way out here."

Chad had to smile, because it wouldn't have surprised him one bit. He was grateful that she'd remained behind, though. It was getting quite late, and she had to get up for work in the morning. That didn't mean he wouldn't have Irish drop him off at her place as planned. He needed to be in her presence after such a potential threat to his life and that of his father's, too.

"Drunk driver?"

"As far as we could tell," Miles chipped in, walking around the front of the tow truck. It had been quite an emotional day for the man. Exhaustion was blatantly obvious in his features, and Chad wanted to see him safely home. "Either that or the individual was too busy on his damn cell phone to pay attention to the road. Idiot drivers are a dime a dozen out here."

Miles yanking on the handle of the passenger side door gave the signal to end the discussion. He wanted to get home, and he was done with idle chitchat.

"Guess this means you're going to be my side kick." Irish flashed a smile. "I know I'm good-looking, but don't go getting any ideas. I have my eye on a certain redhead that might actually give me a run for my money."

Chad would have taken time to think of who the hell had red hair in Blyth Lake, but he immediately came up blank and didn't have time to waste on such trivial matters. He caught Irish by the arm before his friend would have opened the driver's side door.

"Irish, Dad truly believes it was either someone drunk or not paying attention." Chad had already made the decision to speak with Mitch, but no cell service out here in the sticks made it rather difficult. "I was watching the road, and I'm telling you that those headlights veered straight for us without any hesitation. There was no correction to their path until I'd already been forced off the road."

Irish didn't reply right away. His gaze was focused on something down the dark road as he mulled over what Chad was suggesting. Technically, he wasn't suggesting anything. He'd laid it out there for his friend to take or leave.

"Who was aware that you would be headed back toward town on this road tonight?"

Chad had already gone over that list, and it would be easier to name who *didn't* know that he and his father had followed Clayton and Wes back into the city for dinner after visiting the cemetery.

"I'll swing by the station in the morning to speak with Mitch." It wasn't like Chad could do anything about what happened right this minute. "Don't mention this to Dad. He's had a hard enough time of it today as it is."

"Dinner didn't go well?"

"It was spent with Wes and Dad trying to convince Clayton to come home after they finish up the current workload of their construction business. It didn't help that Agent Thorne had practically run Clay through the wringer earlier today. He's convinced that the people of Blyth Lake will treat him the same." Chad had purposefully stayed out of that discussion, not wanting to upset their father over his difference of opinion. Clayton shouldn't come back to town. He had worn out his welcome with the townspeople. Too many neighbors would decide that Schaeffer's Contracting & Flooring wasn't trustworthy enough to do business with if he was back with the company. It would only have all of them suffering versus just the oldest sibling. Besides, Clayton already had something lined up in Cleveland. It was a fresh start for him away from Blyth Lake. It was best to leave well enough alone. "I guess Dad thought today of all days would be a good time to play on Clayton's feelings."

"Didn't work out that way, I take it?"

"No, thank God." Chad instinctively pulled out his cell phone to look at the time. There were still no bars lit up on the top left-hand side of his phone. "Could you—"

"Drop you off at Gwen's house?" Irish finished the inquiry as he yanked on the door handle. "It was already in the plans, Schaeffer."

"I know I smell pretty ripe," Chad said, stepping into the tow truck and sliding across the seat until he was positioned squarely in the middle. "But don't you go get any ideas there, Lawyer Man. I'm taken."

"Would you two fools get a move on?" Miles grumbled, lifting the bill of his cap a little higher on his head. "I want to make it home in time for the eleven o'clock news. They got that new weather girl doing the forecast."

GWEN TURNED THE radio down in her Jeep as she slowly drove down her driveway. A mama bunny with a fluffle of her little kits were munching on new grass at the base of one of the oak trees. They'd all frozen in fear at the initial sound of the approaching engine, but Gwen made sure she'd given them a wide berth as she continued down the gravel drive.

She figured she had another hour before Chad arrived, but that would give her time to take a shower and lay out her clothes for tomorrow morning. She had a meeting with Harlan about his retirement plan, which he didn't realize wasn't nearly as diversified as he should have been. His overall portfolio was carrying far too much risk for a mature plan so close to his intended retirement date.

Time had gotten away from her, and she hadn't decorated for Halloween like she'd planned on when she'd first moved in. The holiday arrived on Wednesday, but she doubted any of the neighbor children would come out this way for candy anyway. Most would go into town where the houses were close together and the candy was plentiful. Mitch and Patty had set it up so that families could walk up and down Main Street, visiting the various shops to gather candy for their bags, as well. At least Beth Ann had seen to it that there were two cornstalks out front of the business with two carved pumpkins to go with them. They had a few cardboard decorations in the window, but that was about the extent of it.

"What the…"

Gwen came to a stop in front of her house. She purposefully didn't turn the wheel to the left, which is what she normally would have done when parking the Jeep.

Something wasn't right.

The porch light was out.

She prided herself on reading situations and adapting to the facts laid out in front of her. Had her return home been uneventful, this wouldn't be anything unusual. She hadn't had time to change the lightbulbs to those energy saver LED ones that last for an obscene amount of years. What she had done was directed the security company to install spotlights to detect movement, thus recording anything or anyone that came onto her property—and those bulbs were currently not activated.

The security lights should have turned on the moment her Jeep came within twenty feet of the house.

Gwen left the Jeep in drive, keeping her foot on the brake. She wanted to be able to make a quick getaway should the need arise. She wasn't a foolish woman, and she certainly wasn't taking any unnecessary chances that could result in her life being cut short.

She pressed the button on the steering wheel that changed her radio display to her contacts. It didn't take her long to choose Mitch's name and connect the call. While she waited for him to answer, she slipped her hand inside her purse for her weapon and checked to make sure she had a round in the chamber. The safety was on. In the service, they called a weapon in this configuration a condition one weapon.

Within a few seconds, the Beretta was fit snug against her palm and ready for action. She checked her mirrors to ensure no one was sneaking up on her, inspecting her blind spots, as well.

"Sis, I can't talk right now. Chester and Stella are fine, but he somehow rammed their vehicle into a utility pole earlier tonight. Half the town is without power, and I can't reach Irish." Mitch muttered a few curse words before answering someone's question that must have been there with him. "Get Byron to run over to his apartment above the garage. He should be there."

Gwen breathed an inaudible sigh of relief so that Mitch couldn't hear it over the speaker. It would explain why her father's house had electricity, but her place didn't. The farmhouse was located on the opposite side of town, though that was only a few miles drive from one end to the other.

"You're not going to find Irish, Mitch." Gwen stored the firearm back into her purse before parking the Jeep. "Chad and Miles were run off the road by a drunk driver. His truck got stuck in a ravine, so Irish headed out that way to give them a tow back to town. I figure they're around forty-five minutes out, give or take the time it took to do the recovery."

"Son of a bitch."

Mitch began relaying her message to whoever was on the scene, but Gwen wasn't going to keep him any longer than necessary.

"Mitch, go take care of Chester and Stella." Gwen let the engine idle while she finished up the call. "And for Christ's sake, get the electric company out there to fix that pole. I don't want to be stumbling around in the dark for the rest of the night."

Gwen severed their connection before Mitch could ask her why she'd called him in the first place. She didn't want him to think she couldn't handle things on her own or else she'd be coddled by him until she was in her nineties. That wasn't going to happen, because she planned on beating her brothers at shuffleboard when they were old, grey, and hunch-backed.

She turned off the key in the ignition, cutting the engine.

With a flick of her wrist, she was able to get the dome light to illuminate the interior of the Jeep. She dug out the small pad of paper she'd been keeping the list of items needed done at the house, taking time to add the generator.

Jace was a really big advocate of having a full-sized generator that ran on natural gas, but most rural areas had very limited access to natural gas service in this part of the country. Any generator would sure as hell come in handy tonight. The backup battery on her sump pump in the basement would only last so long.

After thinking of a few other things to add, she finally clicked the pen and shoved both the writing utensil and pad back into her purse. She removed her weapon more for psychological security than anything else. She couldn't be too careful. There was a valid reason her house had been descended into darkness…and it had nothing to do with the serial killer that had plagued her hometown for far too long. Caution was important, and she had been trained to always be observant of her surroundings.

Gwen reached into the glove compartment for the flashlight she kept on top of her registration and insurance papers. Once she had everything in the proper grip, she exited the Jeep before pressing the button on the key fob. The vehicle's alarm echoed throughout the still of the night, most likely giving the wildlife a brief start.

Sure enough, there weren't any crickets to be heard once the ringing in her ears began to fade.

A gust of wind came from the western field.

Damn, it was getting cold early this year.

Gwen quickly made her way up the porch steps. She held the flashlight in between her teeth as she steadied the beam on the deadbolt. It didn't take long to slip the key into the slot and disengage the bolt. She did the same with the doorknob, finally welcoming the warmth of the house.

The electricity couldn't have been out for too long. Her father had thought she was crazy, but she'd already set the heat to come on at night for a comfortable seventy degrees. Her decision to do so was probably the only reason her house didn't feel like the inside of a refrigerator right now.

Gwen used the heel of her knee-high boot to close the door behind her. She set her purse and keys down on the small table she'd tucked against the wall, still waiting for the large ceramic bowl she'd ordered online. It should arrive tomorrow, along with the throw pillows she'd purchased to add a bit of color to the living room.

The faint fragrance of pumpkin spice filled the air, courtesy of the plug-ins she'd strategically placed throughout the house. She doubted she would have time to bake this fall, and the delicious scent reminded her of Mary Kendall's homemade pumpkin pies. They would normally have had that for dessert at dinner tonight instead of apple pie, but her mother's recipe was missing from her recipe box when Gwen had gone looking for it.

Gwen kept the beam steady in front of her as she slowly made her way into the kitchen. One of the kitchen boxes she'd unpacked the other day had been her previous junk drawer. It was a rather well-organized junk drawer, but it still had an assortment of items...such as extended lighters she used for the various candles she had around the house.

The ringing of her cell phone coming from the living room had her using a few more epithets than her brother had. Then again, he hadn't been in a dark house that could have been written into a horror movie. She promised herself that wouldn't be the case once she did all the upgrades and the exterior was brought up to her satisfaction.

Gwen snatched the lighter from right where she'd left it, closing the drawer with her hip. She did take time to store her weapon in the small of her back at the waistline of her jeans. She really should get her holster out of the closet, but having a weapon on her during normal business hours wasn't so conducive when speaking with clients.

She made her way back into the living room, but the call must have gone to voicemail. It was no doubt Chad, calling to tell her that he was on his way. She'd call him back in a few minutes, after she lit a few candles so that she didn't have to continually hold the flashlight. It didn't take her long, and she'd even gone into the bathroom on the main level to light a smaller candle she'd set on the back of the toilet.

There.

The downstairs was done, but the upstairs could wait until she spoke with Chad. With him being back in cell phone range, Mitch had no doubt gotten ahold of Irish. She could still relay the message regarding Chester and Stella's slight mishap with the utility pole.

Gwen rounded the corner from the bathroom off of the kitchen, carefully making her way into the living room when she came up short. She forced herself to blink, her instincts reverting back to her time in the service.

A dark silhouette shifted slightly in front of a candle—the only candle left burning—making it impossible to tell who was standing in the middle of her living room. The shadows had all but contoured the front of the male figure, but she instinctively recognized that it wasn't Chad or any of her brothers. This intruder had obviously been blowing out the candles she'd lit, thus making it almost impossible for her to make out his identity.

"I'll give you three seconds to head for the door," Gwen said softly, though doing her best to keep her voice steady. She would show no fear. It didn't matter that her heartrate had accelerated, perspiration had coated her body, and adrenaline was now pumping through her veins. The training she'd undergone in the military allowed for adrenaline spikes and stress while still completing the mission—and her goal was clear. "If you don't leave, I'll be forced to kill you."

Gwen had already scanned his silhouette for any indication of a weapon, seeing nothing but his fingers dangling at his sides. That didn't mean anything in this standoff, other than she might have a second or more advantage. She wouldn't waste the time given to her, either.

"Three."

Gwen ever so slowly inched her arm behind her, finally able to even out her breathing once her palm slid over the pistol grip of her Beretta.

"Two."

She was able to ease the weapon out of the waistband of her jeans with practiced simplicity. A hundred scenarios ran through her mind, but she shut them off after three or four. There was no place for doubt in this moment.

It was her life or his, simple as that.

He'd apparently made the decision not to leave, which meant he'd taken the choice out of her hands. She had no intention of dying today, not with everything she had to live for right here in Blyth Lake. There was no time for second-guessing, reservations, or remorse.

"One."

Chapter Twenty-One

"**Y**OU KNOW, THIS could be a sign that you should hire someone," Chad said, lifting his hand in response to his father's goodnight gesture. Irish kept the tow truck idling as they both watched Miles enter his home through the side door. The old man never used the front door, and neither did anyone else that wanted to see him. For all Chad knew, the damn thing had been painted shut years ago. "Even Delaney had Murray Jones helping him out on these late-night calls, though I'll admit they're probably few and far between. And mostly in the winter."

"I thought about hiring one of the Keller boys, but who knows if I'd have any tools in the shop come the next morning." Irish carefully drove around the driveway and out onto the road, still needing to drop Chad off at Gwen's house. After that, he needed to take Chad's truck back to the shop, unhook it from the tow rigging, and then head out to collect Chester's car. "I've heard about their reputation for sticky fingers."

"No worse than mine back in the day," Chad admitted, thinking back to his misspent youth. "They're good kids, Irish. They're just teens living in a small town with nothing to do. They need a firm hand and some discipline."

"Don't you dare tell me those boys are just bored. They could go fishing, hiking, or to the damn movies." Irish came to a stop sign, using the small break to rub his tired eyes. He hadn't been the same since coming out to the town about being a lawyer in his past life or that his sister had been one of the victims in the lake. "Honestly, it's one of the reasons I thought about hiring one of them...or both. They can learn to change oil, rotate tires, or restore old cars. It would at least keep their asses out of trouble."

"Are you getting soft on me in your old age, Irish?"

Chad waited for some quick-witted reply by trying to reach Gwen once more. He'd tried a couple of times ever since they'd gotten into cell phone service range, but she hadn't picked up. Irish had suggested that maybe she was still over at her dad's place, but it was pretty late. More than likely, she'd fallen asleep on the couch or was in the shower.

"You don't think about having kids?"

Okay, this sure as hell wasn't the quick-witted reply Chad had been expecting. The line had already connected to Gwen's voicemail, so he ended the call and studied Irish to see where this conversation was headed.

"It's crossed my mind a time or two," Chad confessed, resting an elbow against the window. It was rare that either one of them ventured into this type of territory, usually keeping things casual on the surface. It was easier like that. "I mean, it's not like either of us are getting any younger."

"Enough kidding around. Is she the one?"

Chad didn't ask Irish to clarify on the *she*. There was only one *she* in his life—Gwen Kendall.

"I didn't go looking for Gwen," Chad revealed, using his cell phone to rub his chin as he pondered on the direction his life had taken recently. This was the type of conversation he should be having with his brothers, but that would happen. Honestly, Irish was as close to a brother as Chad had ever gotten. "She pulled up in that red Jeep as if I'd ordered the perfect woman on Amazon Prime. There isn't one thing I would change about her, Irish."

They rode through town in silence, both of them lost in their own thoughts.

"Chester must have done a number on that utility pole," Irish muttered, entering the back half of town and taking the side road that would lead to Gwen's farmhouse. "If you want, I can take you and Gwen back to your place. The west side of town seems to have electricity."

Chad was already shaking his head, figuring the electric company would be onsite and have things up and running soon.

"Nah, don't worry about it. Mitch is probably chomping at the bit as it is." Chad breathed a sigh of relief when Irish slowly drove down Gwen's long driveway. Her red Jeep shone brightly in the headlights of the tow truck. "See? Gwen came home, so we can always take her Jeep over to my house if need be."

Maybe that wasn't such a bad idea, given that the entire house had been descended into darkness. The clouds overhead had gathered enough to edge out the moonlight for the most part, though every once in a while a beam or two made it through to the ground.

"Roger that." Irish carefully maneuvered the tow truck so that he could easily drive around the gravel circle without having to reverse. "I'll give you a call tomorrow with the damage estimate."

Chad wasn't sure he wanted to know what the damages were to his truck, but it wasn't like he could go without a vehicle for any stretch of time.

"I get the friend's discount, right?"

Irish just laughed, so Chad slammed the passenger door shut. He smacked his palm on the side of the tow truck, giving Irish the all clear that he could pull out. Chad didn't waste time and was on the porch in just a few giant steps. He pulled out his keyring, having already taken off the truck key to give to Irish.

There was one problem.

The front door wasn't locked.

Gwen had the habit of locking everything and anything, most likely acquiring that irritating habit from her time in the military. This was Smalltown, USA. No one ever locked any of their doors. That was until recently. Now everyone and their mother were locking all their doors, windows, and anything else that had the ability to keep a killer at bay.

Chad turned the doorknob, giving a slight push to the wood so that he wasn't directly on the threshold in case he needed to react. He wasn't one of the Kendall boys, having served in the Marines. Chad owned a rifle or two, but he had never needed a handgun. That didn't mean he was without common sense.

He purposefully didn't call out Gwen's name. There was no way she wouldn't have noticed the headlights coming through the various windows at the front of the house. Maybe it was time she got a dog.

Had Gwen simply forgotten to lock the front door? Was she upstairs in the shower or perhaps taking a bubble bath to chase away the chill that had settled in the old house?

A candle flickered on the entry table she'd positioned by the door. It gave off a bit of light, but not enough for him to have a clear view past eight feet. The arch between the living room and the kitchen was pitch black.

He shot a glance toward the staircase, but it faded into the shadows after three steps.

It was then he realized that the only sound he could hear in the stillness was his own uneven breathing. There was no jangling of pipes to indicate that water was running, no swish of moving water from upstairs, and absolutely no reverberation that signified someone was in the house.

It was as if the home had been abandoned once more.

A decision had to be made, though he did have to fight against his instinct to instantly seek out Gwen. Something was wrong. He could feel it eating away at his gut, but he wouldn't be foolish enough to put her in danger.

Chad made sure to look in both directions as he quickly accessed his phone that was still in his grip. He didn't like the sense of being unprotected out in the open, so he took a step over the metal plate and allowed the screened door to quietly close behind him.

"Kendall."

"Mitch, you need to get out to Gwen's place. Now."

Chad didn't wait for Mitch to reply. He disconnected the call and used his phone as a flashlight, which was only slight better than the candle for a source of light. He still reached out to touch the glass jar. It was hot as hell, which meant that Gwen had lit it some time ago. She'd been here a while.

He saw the evidence that everything wasn't okay almost immediately—there was a bullet hole in the wooden frame of the door and a shell casing on the floor.

Son of a bitch.

Chad once again had to fight the inherent need to scream her name.

She'd discharged her weapon right here. There was no way in hell she would have done so if she hadn't been in fear of her life. The smell of expended gunpowder had faded to almost nothing.

With every step he took, he continued to listen intently for any indication that Gwen was nearby. He was half expecting to find her lifeless body lying on the floor, but he prayed to the contrary. She was everything he wanted in his future, and he couldn't accept that she had been taken away from him.

Chad made it as far as the kitchen, stopping long enough to weigh the odds that whoever she'd shot at had gotten the upper hand. Had she been taken upstairs? He couldn't recall seeing anything out on the front porch that would indicate a struggle or a body being dragged.

Once again, he was faced with a decision. Did he retreat and begin looking outside? Did he retrace his steps to the stairway and take a look around upstairs? Or did he continue into the kitchen?

The choice was made for him.

Directly in front of him in the kitchen was the sound of something metal scraping the floor. Before he could react, there was literally a brilliant flash of light...a split second before the piercing sound of a weapon being fired reached his ears.

Chapter Twenty-Two

G WEN HAD GIVEN the man to the count of three. No law
enforcement agency in this country could accuse her of
killing an intruder without giving him a chance to walk away
before she fired her weapon. Castle doctrine stated that she
wasn't required to retreat inside her own home, and he certainly
qualified as an imminent threat to her life. Technically, she
wouldn't have pulled the trigger had the man not shifted in her
direction.

But he *had* moved.

And she discharged her weapon.

There was no doubt that she hit her target, but it had most
likely been a graze because of the way he'd shifted the bulk of
his upper body at the last second. Also, the fact that he slammed
into her as if he was a pro-bowl defensive back and she was the
opposing team's quarterback hadn't quite been fully expected.

Her head had immediately snapped back and hit the tiled
floor of the kitchen. All the oxygen had been forced out of her
lungs, making it all but impossible for her to draw in any air. The
blood that had been pumping through her veins with breakneck
speed could now be heard rushing in her ears, although it was
rather faint against the thunderous ringing left behind by the
discharge of her weapon.

The man recovered faster than she could, thereby giving him
the upper hand. She still had the wherewithal to try and make

out his features, but he'd moved to the right of her. She could only make out his shoulders, and he wasn't as thick as she'd originally surmised.

What was he doing?

It took her a moment to figure out that he was trying to locate her firearm. The force of the fall had knocked it out of her hand when she'd tried to protect herself from his falling weight.

No matter the cost, she had to reach her Beretta before he got the chance.

She struggled to draw air back into her lungs. The horrid wheezing sound wasn't something she'd soon forget. She tried her best to roll over, maybe try and gain some advantage.

The man was far too heavy on top of her torso.

Gwen might not be able to breathe, but she had use of her legs. Granted, she might not have had the most strength, but it was enough to get the job done. She brought her knee up with what little adrenaline she had left, successfully hitting her target square in his junk. Unfortunately, it hadn't been enough to do much damage.

As if by some miracle, the muscles in her throat suddenly opened and allowed for airflow. She dragged in as much oxygen as she could. It was more than evident that he hadn't found her firearm, and she needed to take advantage of this small window of opportunity.

Relying on her training, she pushed all thought out of her mind and used her body as a weapon. She wrapped one leg around his, vying for the advantage. It didn't take her long. This man had no military training. None. She could easily subdue him and…

The edge of the knife cut through her skin as if it were butter.

Gwen didn't have to question what was happening, but the ability to breathe again had given her back another surge of adrenaline. Her body understood what was taking place, but her pain receptors weren't receiving the proper signals. The knife had cut alongside her rib cage with a slashing motion, but the angle in which she'd turned her body had prevented him from stabbing her outright.

Agent Thorne had mentioned that the Blyth Lake Killer didn't use weapons. He strangled his victims. He had an MO that he followed closely, but this certainly wasn't it.

Had the Blyth Lake Killer evolved or was this someone else entirely?

Gwen abruptly released her hold on him and used her arms and legs to shove his upper body up and over. He hadn't been expecting the reversal, so it gave her time to roll over and scramble to her hands and feet.

He had a knife. That was a fact that she couldn't undo, but she could even out the playing field. The block of knives she had for the kitchen were near the stove. Only a step away. All she had to do was fake one direction and move the short distance to arm herself, and she'd already successfully managed to get to her feet.

Unfortunately, the large hand that wrapped itself around her ankle prevented her from reaching her target. She did the only thing she could. She grabbed the candle sitting in the middle of the island and hurled it down toward the man's body.

The fucker could burn.

He immediately released her, giving her the seconds needed to make it to the stove. She chose the first knife she could get ahold of, but by the time she turned around...the kitchen had descended into total darkness. She heard movement from his side of the kitchen, but not before she'd made it to the other side of the counter and placed the large solid obstacle between them.

Gwen went against all instinct and froze, holding her breath so that he couldn't hear her.

He must be doing the same.

The first noise to break the barrier didn't come from the kitchen, though. It was the engine of a large truck. It was Irish bringing Chad home. Neither one of them were aware of the dangers that awaited them hidden in the darkness, and this had now become a cat and mouse game to see who could find the other first.

Gwen didn't have to close her eyes to picture the layout of her new kitchen. She should have open space to launch herself at the man on the floor, but she wasn't so sure he was there anymore.

Little by little, the piercing pain in her side began to make itself known.

She bit her lip to suppress the agonizing moan that wanted to escape. She had no choice but to use the darkness to her advantage, so she slowly lowered herself back down to the floor. If only she could reach the back door. She'd make a run for it, though that did go against her nature.

Still, that idea was the smartest plan she could implement, given the circumstances. She'd also be able to warn Chad before he…

Had the front door just opened?

Shit.

Chad was already inside the house.

And Irish had left from the soft rumbling sound of the re-treating engine.

Gwen wasn't about to go out the back and leave Chad as some kind of sacrificial lamb. He had no idea what waited for him inside, which meant she needed to give him fair warning. Unfortunately, doing so would let this scumbag know her exact location.

There had to be a way out of this.

Gwen did close her eyes this time, willing her body to keep moving. Blood had coated her sweater and the upper part of her jeans. She couldn't risk stopping for a towel, so she slowly and silently released another unsteady breath as she took a step to her left. She would inch toward the living room instead of the back door. It would be harder for this man to defend against two people. She winced at the sudden clatter of metal skidding slightly on the kitchen tile.

Her firearm.

There was no time to think over the situation. She had no choice but to react, because he would do the same. A part of her mind registered the small, brilliant LED cell that shed a pitifully miniscule amount of light for the strength of its source. Chad must be just outside the kitchen doorway, but there wasn't enough light to illuminate the dark shadows of the large kitchen.

Gwen did the only thing she could.

She all but lunged toward the floor, doing her best to keep ahold of the knife as she used her left hand to sweep the floor. It was an unconscious gesture. The pain in her side was becoming almost unbearable, but she refused to let that stop her knowing full well she or Chad could be the next victim to die at the hands of a serial killer.

To Gwen's relief, her fingers touched the cool metal of her firearm. She wasn't a lefty, but she could damn well shoot weak-handed good enough to hit a man-sized target at this range.

She didn't hesitate.

She lifted her weapon toward the rapid shuffle of footsteps, struggling through the pain to identify the direction. Was he coming toward her? Was he running away from her toward the backdoor?

Gwen had a split second to decide if he was about to attack again.

She refused to be any more of a victim than he'd already made her. Any hesitancy could be at the cost of her or Chad's life.

For the second time that evening, Gwen squeezed the trigger on her Beretta.

"GWEN!"

A ringing had set up residence in Chad's ears from the discharge of the pistol, but that didn't prevent him from holding the phone in front of him to locate the one woman who had all but turned his life upside down.

"Gwen!"

"Back door. He went out the back door!"

Chad searched in the direction of Gwen's voice, finally finding her on the tiled floor between the island and the refrigerator.

"Are you—"

Chad went to kneel when she all but forced herself to stand. She barked another order before he could ascertain the problem.

"Chad, go! He went out the back door." Gwen's last word was basically a hiss, and he didn't need to be a doctor to know the sound of pain. "I'll follow behind if—"

Multiple things happened at once to prevent Chad from leaving her side. The distant sound of sirens cut through the air at the same time the motor of the refrigerator began to hum. The overhead light above the sink flickered twice before remaining on, allowing Chad to see…

"What the fuck happened?"

Chad didn't stop to think. He instinctively put down both his phone and the firearm she'd forced into his hand. He quickly opened the drawer that contained the hand towels to use them as bandages for her wound.

"You can't do that," Gwen argued, squinting her eyes against the light as she focused on the back door. "Chad, listen to me. He went out the back—"

Car doors and shouts could now be heard from out front, cutting off Gwen's lecture about the man who attacked her. Chad didn't give a shit what transpired before, but there was no way in hell he was leaving her side now.

"Mitch can send his deputies. Gwen, you're bleeding badly." Chad ignored Gwen's attempt at shoving him away. The amount of blood she'd lost told him that she wouldn't be standing on her feet for much longer, anyway. "I'm not leaving you."

Heavy footsteps up the porch and into the house finally made it into the kitchen, but Gwen saw to it that they kept moving.

"He went out the back door, Mitch," Grace managed to say before tilting her head back as she tried to breathe through the pain. Chad slowly eased her down to the floor, not caring what Mitch or the other deputies did…as long as they called for an ambulance. "He has a knife. No firearm. Maybe five eleven and lean. Short hair."

Mitch must have given a signal, because nearly every individual he'd brought with him left the house quickly and efficiently searching for the man who had only moments before attacked her.

Chad maintained pressure on the dishtowel over the long knife wound down Gwen's side, astounded that she was able to give Mitch all that information without batting an eye. He glanced up from what he was doing to see that her features had pretty much lost all the color she had left. How she was still conscious was beyond him.

"Take care of her." Mitch took a moment to rest a hand on Chad's shoulder. "Julie should be here in a minute."

And just like that, Mitch was gone. Chad and Gwen weren't left alone in the kitchen, though. One man remained behind, though he wasn't one of Blyth Lake's deputies. He most likely belonged on Agent Thorne's team of federal agents.

Chad didn't care who stayed behind. He was glad that Julie was on duty and not Billy Stanton, but honestly anyone with medical expertise would do in this moment.

"Chad, I'm fine," Gwen said, trying to muster up a smile. She failed miserably. "Damn, that hurts."

"You're not fine." Chad had been kneeling, but his knees finally gave out. He sat on his ass while continuing to apply pressure, all the while ignoring the fact that his hands were shaking and covered in her blood. "You've been stabbed, Gwen."

"No, the knife missed and only sliced my side open. There's a big difference." Gwen squeezed her eyes closed as another wave of pain must have washed over her. Chad hated the experience of feeling helpless, but there wasn't a damn thing he could do right now to help her. Anger began to simmer below the surface. "A few stitches, and I'll be—"

"Don't." Chad couldn't take any more of her rhetoric. He'd had enough. "You're hurt, Gwen. You could have fucking died."

"But I didn't." Chad hadn't realized that he'd taken his eyes off her face, most likely because he couldn't stand to see her in so much pain. He looked on as she rested her hand gently over his, almost as if she were comforting him. "Chad, I'm fine. Really. I'll even wager the doctor at the hospital will put in less than twenty sutures."

"I'm not going to bet you on…" Chad let his voice trail off, realizing what she was doing. Here she was—the one who was stabbed, trying to reassure him that everything was going to be okay. She was trying to keep him from going into shock. "I'm a civilian, Gwen. I've heard your brothers talk about their experiences in the military, just as I'm sure you have similar tales. But the worst thing I've ever dealt with was a nail through my thumb. This…this is wrong. You're hurt. You're bleeding. You shouldn't be—"

"Making light of the situation?" Gwen asked, resting her head back against the cupboard. She bit her lip. He'd only ever seen her do that once, and that was at his house that very first night when she'd been talking about life choices and her mother. "I really, really don't want to break down in front of Julie. She'll tell everyone in town that I'm a lightweight, and then it might get back to…"

The Blyth Lake Killer.

If Chad had handled this situation differently, maybe the title could have been retired and the man it belonged to behind bars.

"Then I'll make this wager with you," Chad managed to say, willing to give this woman anything she wanted. "Twenty-five sutures."

"There's that much blood, huh?" Gwen didn't bother to look down at the dishtowel fully soaked with her blood. Hell, he'd had to look away. "Well, this certainly wasn't in the playbook."

Chad lifted an arm to tuck a black strand of hair behind her ear. It was really only to give himself something to do, but she tilted her face so that her cheek rested in the palm of his hand.

"I love you, city girl."

He hadn't meant to say those exact words, especially now. That type of declaration was meant to come with flowers, a candlelight dinner, and maybe some soft music in the background.

Shouts of men and women could be heard in a distance as the search for a serial killer continued outside of this very house. The screened door was being opened and then slammed shut, most likely signaling the entrance of the paramedics. Commotion reigned all around them, but all Chad could focus on was the woman who completed him in a way he'd never thought possible.

"That wasn't on my list, either," Gwen whispered, lifting her lashes to reveal those pretty blue eyes of hers.

"Yes, it was. You know it was," Chad managed to say with a straight face. "I penciled it in your planner this morning, but you must have missed it."

Julie came into view with her bag and another medic by her side, but Gwen reached out so that she could grab ahold of his shirt.

"Did you also pencil in my reply?"

"No, that was a pending action item." Chad fought the urge to pull her tight against him. The sudden shift in movement would undoubtedly cause her pain, and what she needed most was medical attention. He reminded himself that she was going to be okay and they had a long future ahead of them. "We can talk after Julie transports you to the hospital."

"But—"

"Gwen Kendall, this is not how I thought I'd welcome you home."

Chad shifted to the side so that Julie could take ahold of the stained dishtowel, destined to be thrown away after this. He covered his mouth with his hand so that Gwen didn't see the pulling of his lips as he attempted to compose himself.

He could have lost her tonight.

It was an overwhelming thought, and one he couldn't dwell on right this moment. The only thing that mattered was that Gwen had survived and hadn't been added to the victim count of a psychopath who'd terrorized Blyth Lake for far too long.

He was done sitting on the sidelines. He might be a civilian, but he could damn well defend himself and those he loved. It was time for this town to band together to flush out the evil that had existed among them for far too long. He reached for the weapon Gwen had pushed into his hands only moments ago.

Chapter Twenty-Three

GWEN QUICKLY SLIPPED her laptop underneath the covers. She winced as the twenty-six stitches in her side pulled a bit as she turned on her left side and let her head sink into the pillow. She had been told by the ER doctor that she should rest easy today, but that was rather hard when she was the only one who could trade for her clients at the moment.

Low murmurs of several voices traveled up the stairs, but the muffled conversations weren't enough to camouflage Chad's footsteps coming down the hallway. She forced herself to keep her eyes closed, not wanting him to catch her working instead of following the doctor's orders.

She understood his concern, but she really was okay…well, physically. Mentally she was berating herself for letting the Blyth Lake Killer escape when she'd been so close to taking him down. It turned out that she *had* hit her target like she'd thought, but it had only been a graze. Agent Thorne had one of his forensic people remove the bullet from the doorframe in her living room. It was currently being sent to the FBI forensics lab for DNA testing.

Would there be enough DNA on the bullet to make an identification? The amount of blood required was incredibly tiny, but the sample had been superheated by the bullet.

"Did you think I wouldn't catch you?"

Gwen popped open her right eye.

"I'm resting."

"So, I'm not going to find your laptop underneath the covers?"

Gwen decided it was best not to answer, but instead to draw his attention to a more important matter.

"Would you please hand me my planner?"

Gwen ignored the sharp look he shot her way as she carefully propped herself up on the pillow. She ran a hand through her hair, hoping that it was tame enough to go downstairs and pay a small visit to her family.

There was something that she needed to do first.

"You don't need your planner or that laptop."

"Yes, I do." Gwen gave him a smile of innocence. "If you don't go get it for me, you'll force me to get out of bed and retrieve it myself."

"Like I don't know you're thinking about walking downstairs right now," Chad muttered, walking over to the leather bag he'd brought in from her Jeep after they'd gotten home from the hospital. "Stubborn, pigheaded, obstinate, tena—"

He most likely would have continued on like a thesaurus, but her plan to make him speechless had worked.

Last night, hearing those three words he'd uttered at a time when she'd been so close to breaking down had been a gift that she would treasure for the rest of her life. She hadn't been given the chance to respond, but she was doing so now. She didn't want to wait for everyone to leave, because their days hadn't exactly been going as planned.

It was a good thing she jotted down her daily goals in pencil, though Chad was currently staring at the letters she'd written in black ink.

"What does it say I have to do at one-thirty this afternoon?" Gwen asked, having planned this down to the second. She'd noticed since zero eight hundred that he'd been checking on her every half hour...to the minute. The digital clock on her bedside read thirteen hundred hours. "It should be written on there."

"Tell Chad Schaefer that I love him." Chad read the words aloud, his voice thick with emotion. He cleared his throat as he continued making his way to the bed. "This is written in ink."

"Yes, it is." Gwen scooted over an inch so that he could sit with her on the bed. She did her best not to wince at the slight discomfort, knowing full well he'd fawn all over her and attempt to get her to stay in bed for the rest of the day. She leaned forward until her lips were inches from his. "I love you, Chad Schaeffer."

"Are you sure that you don't want to be with one of those city boys your mother used to brag about?" Chad asked, resting his forehead against hers.

"*This* was my mother's dream. And mine, since you asked." Gwen closed her eyes and savored the warmth of his lips when he pressed them against hers. He tasted of coffee. She wanted more, but her family was downstairs. Besides, they had all the time in the world. "And who would finish my list of things to do to the house?"

Chad's shoulders rocked when he tried to stop his laughter.

"Seriously, it's a never-ending list. You might as well move in and reap the benefits of your handiwork."

"Oops." Lance was standing in the doorway with his hands up in surrender. "Sorry. You were taking so long we thought there might be something wrong."

"He's the baby of the family," Gwen explained with an apologetic expression, taking another kiss from Chad before shooing him off the bed. She did take his hand for some leverage as she climbed off the mattress, grateful that she'd worn a pair of shorts and t-shirt to bed last night. "He never did have any patience to speak of."

"Gwen, maybe you should—"

She stood on her tiptoes and pressed her lips to his. She didn't want to hear him say she should be an invalid. That wasn't going to happen, but that didn't mean he couldn't wait on her hand and foot. She deepened their kiss, lifting her left arm around his neck while minding her right.

"You win," Lance declared, backing up and heading down the hallway. "I'm out."

"What I'd really like is some coffee," Gwen whispered, looking up at Chad to force him to see that she was okay. "Please."

Chad sighed in acceptance, tossing the planner on the bed. It landed with a thud, right on top of her laptop that she'd stuffed underneath the comforter. She didn't have to glance up at him to know that he was shooting daggers her way.

"And maybe one of those pain tablets the doc gave us last night."

"That's cheating," Chad berated, letting her take him by the hand anyway and guide him down the stairs behind Lance. The delicious smell of bacon became stronger with each step. "One hour. Then back to bed."

"Only if you join me," Gwen replied, raising her eyebrows up and down in unison as she teased about what the afternoon could hold. He'd given her one hour, and she would make the best of it. There was information she wanted from one person in particular. "Where's Mitch?"

"Mitch is outside on the phone," Gus replied, coming over to Gwen and gently kissing her forehead. "How are you doing, pipsqueak?"

"I'm fine, Dad. Just a few stitches." Gwen tensed a bit, wondering if Chad would let her get away with understating her wound. The stroke of his hand leaving her back as he walked over to the coffee pot had her breathing a bit easier. "I just wish my aim had been a bit better."

"From the sound of it, your aim was just fine. He shifted at the last second, but you still managed to clip him." Jace was sitting on one of the barstools that she'd ordered and expected to receive this morning. Chad must have put them together, and the cream cushions looked exceptional against the oak wood. "Let's hope forensics can pull some DNA on the slug."

"How long is Agent Thorne expecting that to take?" Gwen asked, shaking her head when Shae was going to slide off her stool. "I need to stand a bit, Shae. But thank you."

Chad set a hot cup of coffee in front of her with a floating ice cube shrinking into nothing rather quickly, all the while standing close enough that his warmth soaked into her. She rested her left hip against him in comfort, not missing the small white oval pill he'd set alongside the mug.

"A couple of weeks, maybe more depending on the size of the sample," Mitch responded, turning everyone's head as he joined them in the kitchen. "How are you feeling, sis?"

"Angry that he got away," Gwen answered honestly, scanning the faces of her family. Her father's wrinkles were a little deeper than yesterday, while Noah was being way too quiet standing in the corner of the kitchen. Lance was at the stove making eggs and bacon, while Brynn was at the refrigerator pulling out the orange juice. Reese was setting the table, though it wasn't big enough to seat all of her siblings and their significant others. That would explain the plates on the counter, but more importantly, it signified that they'd all banded together once more. "Tell me you found something, Mitch."

"Nothing we don't already know." Mitch had walked to the other end of the island and leaned his palms against the granite. "The perp knows this area like the back of his hand. We've pieced together from what Chad told us about his hit and run that it was done on purpose. Unless a person is from the area, he or she would not know about the dead zone about an hour out from here. Delaying his return to town was done with intent, just as was Chester and Sheila's accident. Their vehicle was run off the road and into the utility pole that specifically took out the grid on the east part of town."

"It was the only way he was going to get me to enter the house without being suspicious of the lights being out."

"Exactly," Mitch responded, giving Brynn a smile when she set a glass of orange juice in front of him. "You contacted me, I told you the reason for the power outage, and that caused you to feel safe entering your home. All the events leading up to your attack were created with the intent of being able to abduct you without any undue suspicion."

"Why me?" It made no sense. Gwen could see that the others were struggling to find answers. "Didn't Agent Thorne say the profile indicated this psychopath only targets women who aren't happy with their home life? Everyone who knows me knows how much I love each and every one of you."

"Which is why I'm calling in a favor," Mitch confessed, glancing toward the stove. "I got her voicemail, but I'm going to have a friend come out and see if we can get an update on that profile Agent Thorne gave us a few weeks ago."

"I thought your friend couldn't join Agent Thorne's team because of some political issue within the Bureau." Gwen finally picked up the little white pill. The longer she stood, the more her wound began to ache. She needed this time with her family more than she needed her rest. "Has that changed?"

"No, but we'll work around that." Mitch picked up the glass and drained half the contents. "In the meantime, we've taken your description and released it to the press."

"A lot of good that will do you," Gwen muttered, wanting to

close her eyes and enjoy the effects of the white pill. She knew full well that the pain medicine would take at least twenty minutes to reach her system, but the rich coffee made it seem almost instant. "I wasn't able to provide you much. Just height and build. I didn't see his face. He could be one of my neighbors, and I wouldn't know it."

"You provided the police with more information than I could." Shae lifted her cup in a salute. "I wasn't much help at all."

"You both contributed to this investigation," Mitch corrected over the other rebuttals from the rest of the crew. The ringing of his phone signaled that his wait was over. "Go ahead and start eating. I'll join you in a minute."

They all remained silent as Mitch walked out of the kitchen and toward the front door, worry etched in his face much like that of their father. The new sheriff didn't like being made a fool of and it was only a matter of time before retribution was had. Gwen wished she'd been able to dish it out for him, but that chance had passed.

"You'd make me feel better if you'd sit down."

"Then I'll sit," Gwen relented, giving Chad some peace of mind. "But only if you join me."

She had a feeling he'd put together the stools as a way to keep his mind off of what could have been. She hadn't missed the throw pillows placed strategically on the couch in the living room, either. Chad had kept himself busy, but she had other ways to do that for both of them later this afternoon.

There *was* one thing she wanted to put on her schedule tomorrow.

"Dad?"

Gwen reached out to capture his hand when he would have gone to sit at the table. He immediately stopped, and she understood then that he would have given her the world in that moment if he could have.

That's what parents did for their children.

But she had something simpler in mind, and something that was long overdue.

"Maybe after work tomorrow we could take a walk over to the cemetery?" Gwen squeezed his hand, hoping that he'd recognize that she'd finally come to terms with her past decisions. "I'd really like to visit with Mom."

Gus had to swallow a couple of times before answering, but he nodded his head. She was once again rewarded with a kiss on the forehead before he joined the others at the table. It took another minute before she could speak herself.

"Chad?"

"I'm right here, city girl."

Gwen turned around, right into his open embrace. She lifted her left hand, not surprised when he realized that she wanted to ask him something private. He leaned down closer, searching her gaze to give him some idea of what she was about to say.

"Did you happen to look at the time I blocked out in the planner for later this afternoon?"

"I did," Chad murmured, the warmth of his breath making promises that she fully intended to make sure he kept. "Did I happen to mention I'm getting myself a planner? And every day from here on out is going to include…"

Gwen laughed out loud when Chad continued to let her in on his plans…in colorful detail. All of this could have been taken away from her last night, but fate had seen to it that her family had remained intact. It could very well have been her mother, watching out for all of them from above. It was impossible to know the reason, but there was one irrefutable fact—Gwen was finally home where she belonged.

~ The End ~

It's hard to believe that the Keys to Love series is coming to an end, but the last book—Unlocking Darkness—will be in your hands soon! Click below for all the exciting details!

www.kennedylayne.com/unlocking-darkness.html

USA Today Bestselling Author Kennedy Layne brings you the thrilling conclusion to the Keys to Love series that will leave you wondering…who can you truly trust?

Mitch Kendall was welcomed home after sixteen years by a murder investigation that plagued every member of his family. He wanted the dark cloud lifted that hung over his return, so he did the only thing he could—he called in a favor from an old friend.

Allie Delaney spent most of her adult life building her career as a special investigator solving cold cases for the New York Police Department. She loves her city and would never consider leaving the bright lights, but she was willing to take a well-deserved vacation to pay back an old friend.

While Mitch and Allie work together to hunt down a rural serial killer, their attraction spirals out of control. As they begin to mix business with an intense pleasure, they draw nearer to a malevolence that has been secreted away for over a decade. They might find themselves wishing the sins of the past had stayed buried when the evil in the darkness reaches out for them.

Books by Kennedy Layne

Office Roulette Series
Means (Office Roulette, Book One)
Motive (Office Roulette, Book Two)
Opportunity (Office Roulette, Book Three)

Keys to Love Series
Unlocking Fear (Keys to Love, Book One)
Unlocking Secrets (Keys to Love, Book Two)
Unlocking Lies (Keys to Love, Book Three)
Unlocking Shadows (Keys to Love, Book Four)
Unlocking Darkness (Keys to Love, Book Five)

Surviving Ashes Series
Essential Beginnings (Surviving Ashes, Book One)
Hidden Ashes (Surviving Ashes, Book Two)
Buried Flames (Surviving Ashes, Book Three)
Endless Flames (Surviving Ashes, Book Four)
Rising Flames (Surviving Ashes, Book Five)

CSA Case Files Series
Captured Innocence (CSA Case Files 1)
Sinful Resurrection (CSA Case Files 2)
Renewed Faith (CSA Case Files 3)
Campaign of Desire (CSA Case Files 4)
Internal Temptation (CSA Case Files 5)
Radiant Surrender (CSA Case Files 6)
Redeem My Heart (CSA Case Files 7)
A Mission of Love (CSA Case Files 8)

Red Starr Series

Starr's Awakening(Red Starr, Book One)
Hearths of Fire (Red Starr, Book Two)
Targets Entangled (Red Starr, Book Three)
Igniting Passion (Red Starr, Book Four)
Untold Devotion (Red Starr, Book Five)
Fulfilling Promises (Red Starr, Book Six)
Fated Identity (Red Starr, Book Seven)
Red's Salvation (Red Starr, Book Eight)

The Safeguard Series

Brutal Obsession (The Safeguard Series, Book One)
Faithful Addiction (The Safeguard Series, Book Two)
Distant Illusions (The Safeguard Series, Book Three)
Casual Impressions (The Safeguard Series, Book Four)
Honest Intentions (The Safeguard Series, Book Five)
Deadly Premonitions (The Safeguard Series, Book Six)

About the Author

First and foremost, I love life. I love that I'm a wife, mother, daughter, sister... and a writer.

I am one of the lucky women in this world who gets to do what makes them happy. As long as I have a cup of coffee (maybe two or three) and my laptop, the stories evolve themselves and I try to do them justice. I draw my inspiration from a retired Marine Master Sergeant that swept me off of my feet and has drawn me into a world that fulfills all of my deepest and darkest desires. Erotic romance, military men, intrigue, with a little bit of kinky chili pepper (his recipe), fill my head and there is nothing more satisfying than making the hero and heroine fulfill their destinies.

Thank you for having joined me on their journeys...

Email:

kennedylayneauthor@gmail.com

Facebook:

facebook.com/kennedy.layne.94

Twitter:

twitter.com/KennedyL_Author

Website:

www.kennedylayne.com

Newsletter:

www.kennedylayne.com/newslettertext.html

www.ingramcontent.com/pod-product-compliance
Lightning Source LLC
Chambersburg PA
CBHW060434180626
46817CB00007B/2815